DISCARD

Date: 3/2/18

LP FIC WEBBER
Webber, Meredith,
Engaged to the doctor sheikh

'Marry you? Am I supposed to leap about in excitement at that thought? Or am I supposed to feel honoured? To be married to such an important man as Sheikh al Askeba!'

Lila thought she was doing quite well—given the total shock Tariq's words had generated. But yelling at him wasn't enough...not when she felt like grinding her teeth or punching something.

But marry *Tariq*—who'd been forced to offer marriage? Not love, just marriage...

Her heart scrunched in her chest. But that was stupid—this was a land where the head ruled the heart, and *his* head had offered marriage.

What alternative did she have?

Leave this place which she'd just discovered for certain was her heritage? Leave the family she'd only just found? The family she'd sought for so many years?

But the alternative was exile!

Could she *really* just walk away?

Dear Reader,

These days so many people seem to be tracing their ancestry, but for Lila the search to find out about her parents is more a search for her own identity. Orphaned at four, in a foreign country, she's had little to guide her in her search: some scraps of music, memories of a box her mother treasured...and the pendant her mother had tied around her neck the day of her accident.

The last thing she expects to find as she follows her tenuous leads is love, but that is the ultimate reward for her tenacity in following the clues to her parents' lives. As you will realise my love affair with sandy desert countries is still strong, and I hope you enjoy the romance of them as much as I do.

This is my second book involving Hallie and Pop's foster family in the little coastal town of Wetherby—the first being Izzy and Mac's story in *A Forever Family for the Army Doc*. And now I've become acquainted with them all there will be two more books to come!

Meredith Webber

ENGAGED
TO THE
DOCTOR SHEIKH

BY
MEREDITH WEBBER

HarperCollins
PUBLISHERS
Since 1817

First published in Great Britain 2017
By Mills & Boon, an imprint of HarperCollins*Publishers*
1 London Bridge Street, London, SE1 9GF

Large Print edition 2017

© 2017 Meredith Webber

ISBN: 978-0-263-06736-1

MIX
Paper from
responsible sources
FSC® C007454

Printed and bound in Great Britain
by CPI Group (UK) Ltd, Croydon, CR0 4YY

Meredith Webber lives on the sunny Gold Coast in Queensland, Australia, but takes regular trips west into the Outback, fossicking for gold or opal. These breaks in the beautiful and sometimes cruel red earth country provide her with an escape from the writing desk and a chance for her mind to roam free—not to mention getting some much-needed exercise. They also supply the kernels of so many stories it's hard for her to stop writing!

Books by Meredith Webber

Mills & Boon Medical Romance

The Halliday Family

A Forever Family for the Army Doc

Wildfire Island Docs

The Man She Could Never Forget
A Sheikh to Capture Her Heart

The Accidental Daddy
The Sheikh Doctor's Bride
The One Man to Heal Her

Visit the Author Profile page
at millsandboon.co.uk for more titles.

CHAPTER ONE

LILA SAT IN the huge jet, surrounded by strangers, all intent on their own lives. Did they all know where they're going or, like her, were they travelling into the unknown?

A shiver started in her stomach at the thought of just how unfamiliar her destination might be, and to divert her mind before she became terrified of what lay ahead, she thought of the family, *her* family, all gathered at the airport to wish her well.

Hallie and Pop, her foster parents, and the gaggle of loved ones she'd grown up with, bonded into sisters and brothers by the love of two wonderful people. There were in-laws now, and nieces and nephews…

True family.

The next plane was smaller, though more luxurious, but it wasn't until she boarded the third flight of what was beginning to seem like a never-ending journey that she met real luxury. Not a big plane by any means, but beautifully appointed, with armchair-like seats, and attentive stewards offering tasty delicacies and tantalising sweets.

The novelty of it kept her going until one of the attendants leant over her to point out the window.

'We are coming in to land at Karuba Airport now and as we circle you will see the rugged mountains, the dunes on the desert plains, and the pink flamingos on the lake. You will see how beautiful our country is, and it will welcome you like a lover.'

The seriousness in the man's eyes—the obvious love of his country shining through the words—told Lila he meant nothing personal in the words.

But a country that would welcome her like a lover?

Poetic, that's what it was!

And poetic was how it looked. Great slabs of rock, thrown by giants, built up into mesas and pyramids, smooth and brown, with glowing green foliage showing in the deep valleys—were they oases? But the flamingo lake eluded her, and the sand she saw was golden brown, not pink.

No, the pink had to be a confused memory—a pink toy on beach sand—it had to be.

The plane kissed the runway, settled, and taxied to a pristine white building, with many domes and minarets, their spires tipped with gold.

A fairy-tale palace for an air terminal?

The passengers disembarked smoothly, moving through a tunnel into the cool air-conditioned building, the usual immigration and customs checks lying ahead.

From her place in the queue, Lila studied her fellow travellers. Some were locals returning home, the women in burkas with bright flashes of pretty clothing visible beneath them. A number of the men wore robes, black decorated with intricate gold embroidery, while others wore beautifully cut and fitted business suits.

A cosmopolitan place, Karuba?

It was her turn at the immigration counter. She

handed over her Australian passport with the completed immigration form and waited while it was examined—and examined again—just as *she* was examined, the man behind the counter looking from her picture to her face as if somehow she'd changed her appearance on the journey.

He studied the immigration document she'd filled in before disembarking, while the people behind her shuffled uneasily in the line, and concern began to bloom in her chest.

Had the official pressed a bell of some kind on his desk, alerting the second man that appeared? Clad in an immaculate dark suit, pristine white shirt and bright red tie, he smiled at her through the window.

Not an especially welcoming smile, but a smile nonetheless.

Not that it eased the concern...

'Dr Halliday, we must speak to you,' he said smoothly—*too* smoothly? 'If you would like to come this way?'

Should she ask why?

Refuse?

She'd just landed in a foreign country and who knew what might be happening?

'Do you need help?' the passenger behind her asked.

'I don't think so. I'm here to work at the hospital. It might be that someone on the staff is waiting to meet me,' she told him. 'But thank you.'

Lila gathered up her carry-on luggage and prepared to follow the man who'd summoned her, he behind the wall of immigration windows, she in front of it.

It's just the hospital doing a special welcome thing, she told herself, but the fingers of her right hand went to the locket she wore around her neck and she twiddled with it as she always did when nervous or uncertain.

'Just through this way,' he said when they came together at the door into a long passage. 'We will not detain you long.'

Detain?

Detain was not a nice word—it had bad connotations—detainees were prisoners, weren't they?

She was shown into a comfortable enough room, and the well-dressed official offered her a chair and sat opposite her.

'You have been to our country before?' he asked, so carefully polite Lila felt a chill of fear feather down her spine.

'Never,' she said. 'I have come to work in the hospital, in the paediatric section. That's my specialty, you see.'

Perhaps she should have added that she thought her parents *might* have come from Karuba, but as everyone at home had told her it was a long shot—all she'd seen was a vaguely familiar box—she decided not to mention it.

The man seemed to be studying her—discreetly enough—but the attention was making her more and more uneasy.

'I have the details of the doctor at the hospital who employed me,' she said. 'Perhaps you would be good enough to contact him for me.'

She dug in her handbag for the email she'd received from the man, confirming her appointment, and as her fingers touched the piece of paper, she remembered just what a presence he had had, even on a fuzzy computer screen.

Tariq al Askeba—either the head of the hospital or head of Paediatrics, she hadn't quite managed to get that straight.

She handed the email to the official, and was surprised to see the frown that immediately gathered his eyebrows.

'You are to work with Sheikh al Askeba?' he demanded.

'Yes, I am,' Lila responded firmly. 'And I'd like you to contact him as soon as possible so he can sort out whatever is going on here.'

The man looked even more upset.

'But he is on his way now,' he said. 'You are perhaps a friend of his?'

'I am about to be his employee,' Lila countered.

'Then he will be able to sort it out,' the man assured her, although his increasing nervousness was now making her very worried indeed.

Fortunately, the worry was diverted when the door to the room opened silently and a tall, regal figure in a snowy white gown, and a black circlet of braid holding an equally white headdress in place, strode in.

An eagle was Lila's first thought. Were there white eagles?

But the deep-set eyes, the slightly hooked nose, the sensuous lips emphasised by the closest of beards told her exactly who it was.

Even on a fuzzy video image, Dr—or Sheikh?—al Askeba had radiated power, but in full regalia he was beyond intimidating—he was magnificent...

Magnificent *and,* if the lines of fatigue around his eyes and bracketing his mouth were anything to go by, exhausted.

She stood, held out her hand and introduced herself. Long, slim fingers touched hers—the lightest of clasps—more from manners than in welcome.

Neither was there welcome in the dark eyes that seemed to see right through her, eyes set beneath arched black brows. Or in the sensuous mouth, more emphasised than hidden by the dark stubble of moustache and chin.

'Dr Halliday, forgive me. I am Tariq al Askeba. I am sorry you have been inconvenienced. I had intended being here to meet you but—well, it's been a long night.'

The words were right—the apology seemed genuine—but the man was studying her closely, confusion now adding to the exhaustion she could read in his face.

He turned to the first man and spoke quickly, musically almost, the notes of the words echoing way back in Lila's memory and bringing unexpected tears to her eyes.

'We have upset you,' he said—demanded?—turning back to her and obviously noticing her distress.

She waved away his protest.

'I'm fine,' she said. 'I'd just like to know what's going on. What am I doing here in this room? Why was I separated from the other travellers?'

She was trying to sound strong and composed but knew her fingers, toying nervously with her pendant, were a dead giveaway.

'If I may,' he said, coming closer to her, all but

overwhelming her with a sense of presence she'd never felt before.

Power?

Why would it be?

He was just a man...

But he reached out his hand, calmed her fidgeting fingers, and lifted the pendant onto his long slim fingers so he could examine it.

She should have wrenched it away from him, or at least objected to him touching it, but he was too close—paralysingly close—and she could feel the warmth from his hand against the skin on her chest.

She tried to breathe deeply, to banish the uneasiness she was feeling, but her breaths were more like pants, so much was he affecting her.

'This is yours?' he asked at last.

'Of course,' she said, and cursed herself for sounding so feeble. 'My mother gave it to me when I was small.'

He straightened, looking down at her, dark eyes searching her face—intent.

Intense!

Bewildered?

'Your mother?'

Once again she, not the pendant, was the focus of his attention, his gaze searing into her, his eyes seeing everything.

And when he spoke, the word—one word— was so softly said she barely heard it.

'Nalini?'

And somewhere through the mists of time, and hurt, and sorrow, the name echoed in her head.

'What did you say?' she whispered, shaking now, totally bewildered by what was going on, terrified that ghosts she'd thought long dead had returned to haunt her.

'Nalini,' he repeated, and she closed her eyes and shook her head.

But closed eyes and a headshake didn't make him go away.

'You know the name,' he insisted, and she lifted her head. Looked into eyes as dark as her own, set in a face that seemed carved from the same rock as the mountains she'd seen from the plane.

Had he hypnotised her so that she answered?

Hesitantly—the words limping out—thick with emotion...

'It might have been my mother's name. It *might* have been! The police asked again and again, after the accident in Australia, but I didn't know it. I was too young.'

Her body felt as if it was breaking into pieces, but as clear as the voices of the two men present she could hear another man's voice calling, 'Come, my lovely Nalini, come.'

They were at a beach, she could see it clearly, her father paddling in the waves, calling to Nalini...

Her father's voice?

It *was* her mother's name!

Had her interrogator sensed her despair, that he released the pendant and rested his hand on her shoulder? Heat radiated from the light touch of his palm.

'Your mother is dead?'

The question was asked softly, gently, but he'd gone too far.

She'd been so excited when she'd finally found

the name 'of the country she believed to be her mother's that she'd pushed madly on with her quest, getting a job and making arrangements to go there. Travelling outside Australia for the first time in her life, to a place she'd only recently heard of, and might yet prove wrong. But to be treated like this, with—yes—suspicion of some kind on her arrival, with no explanation or excuse, it was just too much.

'Look,' she said, standing up to give herself more presence, although at five feet five that didn't amount to much, 'I have come here as a guest worker in your country with all the proper documentation and I have no idea why I'm being held here. I want to know what's going on and I'd like to see my consul, please, and you might ask him to bring a lawyer.'

The Sheikh stepped back but she knew he wasn't giving way to her—he was far too authoritative, too controlled.

'I'm sorry,' he said, 'please, sit down again. I can explain, but perhaps some refreshments… You would like tea, coffee, a cool drink?'

Without waiting for a reply, he waved the other man from the room, giving an almost inaudible command that obviously would produce a variety of refreshment.

'It is the locket, you see,' he said, sitting opposite her as she sank into the chair, knees weakened by her momentary rebellion. 'The immigration official recognised it. I would need to examine it to be sure, but it is very like a piece of jewellery that, among other pieces, went missing from the palace many years ago.'

Lila's fingers felt for it again, remembering the familiar shape—the comforting shape—of it.

But his words were playing on a loop in her head. His words, and a hint of…menace, surely not—in his voice.

'Missing?' she queried, and he paused, then was saved from answering by the first man reappearing, followed by two women bearing trays, one with a coffee pot, teapot, cups and saucers, and a selection of cold drinks on it, while the other carried a tray with an array of food from tiny sandwiches to olives and cheeses and fruit.

'Please,' her new boss said, waving his hand at the trays on the table. 'Help yourself.'

Does he really expect me to eat? Lila wondered.

Has he no idea just how knotted my stomach is?

How terrified I am?

'I would rather finish whatever is going on here,' she said, hoping she sounded firmer than she felt. 'You are making me feel like a criminal when I have done nothing wrong.'

Okay, so the last words had come out a little wobbly and she'd had to swallow hard before she could get them said at all, but behind the polite façade of the two men in the room she could sense a tension—a danger?—she couldn't fathom.

'May I see the locket again?'

He reached his hand towards her, non-threatening words but a command in his tone.

'I don't take it off,' she said, unwilling to be pushed further.

Stubborn now!

'It was my mother's last gift to me. About the only thing I remember from that day—the day my parents died—was my mother fastening it around my neck, telling me it was mine now, telling me it would protect me—my Ta'-wiz.'

Her fingers clung to it, hiding it from the stranger's curious eyes.

'They both died?'

Dr—Sheikh?—al Askeba's words were gentle but Lila refused to let them sneak under her defences. She'd told the story before and she could tell it again—dry eyed, the anguish that had never left her hidden behind the mask of time.

'In a car accident. The car caught fire, a truck driver who saw it happen pulled me from my seat in the back before the car exploded.'

'And you were how old?'

Lila shook her head.

'We guessed four—my new family and I—but we never knew for certain.'

'And your mother's name was Nalini?'

More worried now the conversation had turned

so personal, Lila could only nod, although she did add, 'I think so, but I had forgotten.'

The words caught at her and she raised despairing eyes to the stranger.

'How could I have forgotten my own mother's name? How could I not have remembered? Yet when you said it I saw her in my mind's eye.'

She closed her eyes, more to catch wayward tears than to keep the image there.

Then cool fingers touched hers, easing them just slightly from the locket. She felt it lifted from where it lay against her skin, heard his small gasp of surprise.

'You were burned?'

'The car caught fire.'

'And the locket burnt your skin—some protection!'

'No, *I* survived!' Lila reminded him, angered by his closeness—his intrusion into her life. 'It *did* protect me.'

But now he'd grasped her fingers, turning them to see the faint scars at the tips there as well.

'You kept hold of it?'

The words were barely spoken, more a murmur to himself, then he squeezed her fingers and released them, stepped back, apologising again for the inconvenience, adding, 'I had rooms arranged for you at the hospital, a small serviced apartment close to a restaurant on the ground floor, but I think for now you should stay at the palace. You will be safe there, and maybe you can help us solve an old mystery.'

'Palace?' Lila whispered. 'No, I'll be very happy in an apartment at the hospital. The sooner I get settled the sooner I can make it a home. I'm sorry, I have no idea what's going on but whatever it is I don't like it, not one little bit.'

He smiled at her then, the exhausted stranger with the even stranger ways.

'Perhaps you are home, Nalini's daughter, perhaps you *are* home.'

Tariq knew he was staring. Not openly, he hoped, but darting glances at the young woman who was so like the one he'd loved as a child.

He'd been eight, and Nalini had been beautiful, brought into the household because she was Second Mother's sister, to be company for her, someone familiar.

But very quickly she'd become everyone's favourite. Back then she'd been like the Pied Piper from the old European fairy tale and all the children in the palace had followed where she led, laughing with her, playing silly games, being children, really, in a place that had, until then, been rather staid and stolid.

Tariq was pouring coffee as the memories flashed past, handing a cup to their guest, explaining they would be leaving as soon as her luggage had been collected.

She took the cup he offered her and looked up into his face, her almond-shaped brown eyes meeting his, anger flickering in them now.

'And if I don't want to live in the palace?' she asked, steel in her voice as if the tiredness of the long journey and the stresses of her arrival had been put aside and she was ready to fight.

'It need only be temporary but if you are Nalini's daughter then you are family and as family you must stay in our home.'

How could he tell her that things had not gone well for the family since Nalini's—and the locket's—departure and things were getting worse. He was a modern man, yet it seemed imperative that the locket return to the palace where its power might reignite hope and harmony.

Not that she could read his thoughts, for she was still fighting him about his decision.

'Because I'm family? Or because you think my mother stole the locket?' she challenged, setting the tiny cup back on the table. 'What makes you think it was her? For all you know she could have seen it somewhere and bought it! Maybe she *was* from Karuba—*was* the same Nalini you knew—and it reminded her of her home. But stealing from a palace—how could anyone do that?'

Al'ama, she was beautiful, sitting there with anger sparking in her eyes! The simple cream tunic and flowing trousers—loose clothing the hospital advised visiting staff to wear—emphasised rather than hid a shapely body, the colour enhancing the classic purity of her features and lending warmth to the honey-coloured skin.

Not that he could afford to be distracted...

'Nalini lived at the palace because she was family, as you will, if you are family,' he said firmly, as the door opened and a nod from the man beyond it told him they were ready to leave. 'Come, there are more comfortable places where we can discuss this, and probably a better time. You must be weary after your journey, and should rest. Later, we will talk.'

He put out his hand to help her up from the low seat, but she refused it, standing up herself, very straight—defiant...

Tariq cursed himself. He'd handled this badly from the beginning. A long night searching bone-marrow donor registers had led to nothing, then the call from the airport, when what he'd really needed was a few hours' sleep.

So, tired as he was, seeing the woman—a woman called Halliday who looked so like Na-lini—had thrown him completely. He'd been thrust into the past and a time of tension, bitterness and even hatred in the palace.

Added to which, she was wearing the Ta'wiz, the most sacred of the objects that had gone missing at the time of Nalini's disappearance. Customs and immigration officials had been on the lookout for all the jewellery for decades but the Ta'-wiz was the one they all knew best, for the hollowed-out crystal with the elaborate gold-and-silver casing around it was believed to carry the spirit of the people's ancestor.

The immigration officer would not have needed to look closely at it, for he would have felt its power, as Tariq had the moment he'd entered the room, for this simple piece of jewellery was believed to have spiritual qualities—and the strongest of these was protection.

He waved her towards the door, and followed her, looming over her slight form like an evil jinn.

Lila, her name was Lila, he remembered, and right now he wanted to go back in time, to have been at the airport when the plane landed, not finishing a despairing computer search for the magic formula that might save his brother.

He could have greeted her properly, taken her to the hospital, maybe not even noticed the locket around her neck.

The scars on her fingertips told him she'd clung to it as her mother—as both her parents—had died in a flaming inferno. Apart from it being a last gift from her mother, it had protected her, of course she didn't want to take it off.

Neither could he take it from her…

But perhaps with it safely back in the palace— even in the country—some of the uncertainties and ill-fortune of the last decades would diminish and peace could be restored.

He shook away such thoughts. His country had grown from a collection of nomadic villages to a world presence in a matter of decades and his concern was that it had happened too quickly for many people to adjust and the happiness everyone had expected to come with wealth had somehow eluded them.

* * *

Swept along in this surreal dream, Lila followed the man who had first taken her to the small room down more corridors and finally out onto a covered parking area.

A driver in striped trousers and a long striped tunic leapt from the only car parked there, a huge black vehicle, to open the back door, the tail of his turban dropping forward over his shoulder as he bowed towards her.

Uncertainty made Lila look back, but the large man—her new boss—was right behind her, sober-faced but nodding as if her getting into the car was the right thing to do.

Not that she had a choice unless she decided to run straight out into the blinding sunlight and just keep running.

To where?

Home and family, and the only safety she knew, were all a long way off. Besides, she'd come here to find out about her birth family—her parents—about *their* country! So she'd put up with the tall man's bossy ways and just go with the flow.

For the moment!

She tightened her lips then smiled to herself as she imagined her sister Izzy's reaction to such lip-tightening.

'Beware, the quiet one is ready to erupt,' Izzy would have said, and usually laughter would have followed, because Lila *wouldn't* have erupted.

But Izzy wasn't here to laugh her out of it. Izzy was thousands of miles away with a new husband and a new father for her daughter...

And she, Lila, was on her own.

Her fingers crept up to touch the locket, shaking it as if she might be able to hear the tiny grains of sand the kind young woman at the University International Day had put into it for her.

Though not pink sand...

She *knew* there'd been pink sand once...

The man, Dr—Sheikh—al Askeba, was in the vehicle with her now, not close, for the seat was wide enough for four people, but she could feel his presence as a vibrant energy in the air.

'How did you know to come here? To Karuba?

Had your parents told you of it?' he asked, and Lila turned to stare at him—or at his strong profile for he looked not at her but straight ahead, as if someone else might have spoken.

She shook her head.

'I just kept looking,' she said quietly, remembering the dozens of times when something that had seemed like a lead had turned to nothing.

'But with your parents dead how did you know what to look for?'

Now he turned to her, and she saw the question echoed in his eyes. Not an idle question then, not small talk. This man wanted to know, and she guessed that when he wanted something he usually got it.

'I didn't, not really, but sometimes I would hear a note or phrase of music and it would hurt me here.' She pressed her fist against her chest. 'Or I would see something, a design, a colour, that brought my mother's face to mind. I grew up in a small country town so I had to wait until I went to the city to go to university before I could really start looking. But then, with studies and exams...'

'So, it's only recently you discovered something about Karuba?'

Lila smiled.

'You could say that,' she told him, remembering the joy of that particular day. 'From time to time I gave up, then something would remind me and I'd be off again. Two days before I emailed to apply for a job at the hospital here, I heard about an International Student Day at a nearby university.'

'And you went along, listening for a scrap of music, seeking a design, a pattern?'

'You make it sound like a plan,' she said, suddenly wanting him to understand. 'But it was never that, just a—a search, I suppose, a first clue that might lead somewhere else. You see, when the accident happened, the police tried for many months to identify my parents—to find out who they were and where they were from, looking for family for me, I suppose. But all they found were dead ends.'

He nodded as if he understood, but all doctors could do the understanding nod so she didn't put much stock in it.

But when he asked, 'And this last time you looked?' his voice was deepened by emotion, as if he *actually* understood.

Lila smiled with the sheer joy of remembering.

'There were stalls everywhere, but I could hear the music and I followed it. And at one stall, beneath a big tree, I saw a small wooden box with a patterned silver inlay.'

She paused, emotion catching at her throat again.

'Something in the pattern…I mean, I'd seen many boxes over the years but this one took me straight back to my mother, to the little box she had always kept close. Her sand box, she called it. I touched it and the girl—the student—handed it to me.'

'So you asked where it was from?'

Lila nodded.

'At first I couldn't speak, I just held it, felt its warmth, felt my mother's hand on it, my hand on hers. But then I realised that I had the name of the country where my mother might have been born. I had my first real clue.'

CHAPTER TWO

HE SHOULD HAVE let her go, seen her safely to the hospital and forgotten the Ta'wiz, pretended it was just a locket—such things were sold all over the world, like amulets and chains with women's names written in Arabic, pretty tokens and jewellery, rather than sacred objects.

He should forget the laughing Nalini of his youth, and the problems of his people. He should let this woman do her job, serve her twelve months' contract and depart.

From all he'd heard as he'd chased up her references, she was an excellent paediatrician—what more could he ask of her?

But glancing sideways at her as she sat, bolt upright, her head turned to look out the window, her shining dark hair in a loose plait down her back, he knew he could no more have pretended she was just a doctor than he could have walked naked through the shopping mall.

In fact, the second would probably have been easier, because he would have debased only himself, while ignoring this woman's sudden presence in his country would have been…

Traitorous?

He wanted to talk to her, to ask her more, to hear that soft husky voice, but anger at her treatment—deserved anger—was emanating from that straight back.

Until they reached the wide, ceremonial road that led straight to the palace gates.

'Oh, but they're gum trees,' she cried, turning back to look at him, her face alight with surprise and delight. 'Eucalypts—from home!'

And several things clicked into place in Tariq's head.

First was the confirmation that she was beautiful. Not blindingly attractive as Nalini had been, but with a quiet radiance that shone when she smiled.

And secondly, the trees!

Australia!

Two years after Nalini had disappeared, a gift of two hundred eucalypt seedlings had arrived at the palace, packed in boxes in a container, sender unknown. The only clue had been a picture of an avenue of such trees and his father had taken it that they were meant to be planted on the approach to the palace.

Had his father suspected they were a gift from the runaway that he had had the trees tended with more care than new-born babies?

Now they grew straight and tall, and had brought a smile to the face of the newcomer.

A smile so like her mother's it touched something in his chest...

Should he explain—about the disappearance of Nalini, about the trees arriving?

No, it would be too much too soon, although living in the palace she'd hear the gossip soon enough, even if it was close to three decades old.

Although he could explain the trees.

'They were a gift, sent unexpectedly to my father, and he planted them along here.'

That would do for now.

She smiled at him.

'They look great. They obviously like it here. Where I grew up was on the coast and although we had sand, we had rain as well so the trees grew tall and strong. Can you smell them? Smell the scent of the oil? Sometimes at night it filled the air, and especially after being in the city it would tell me I was home.'

'The desert air is like that,' Tariq told her. 'Cities seem to confuse our sense of smell, but once we're out of them it comes back to us, familiar as the sound of the wind blowing sand across the dunes, or the feel of cold spring water in an oasis.'

Lila heard the words as poetry, and stared at the man who'd spoken them. He'd erupted into her life, caught her at a time when anyone would be vulnerable—new job, new country, new customs and language—then confused her with her mother's name.

Seeing the familiar trees had strengthened her, and she decided to go along with whatever was happening, not that she'd had much choice up until now. But she'd come here to find out about her parents, and this man had known her mother.

Had suspected her mother was a thief?

So maybe she *had* to stay in the palace, if only to clear her mother's name…

She turned away, catching a glimpse of a large building at the end of the avenue.

A very large building, not replete with domes and minarets but with solid, high stone walls, earth brown, and towers set into them at regular intervals.

Guard towers? For men with guns?

More a prison than a palace, surely?

Her mother had been a thief?

No, that last was impossible!

She was letting her imagination run away with her, but as they drew closer to the imposing façade, she shivered.

'It is old, built as a fort, not a palace,' her companion explained. 'But inside you will see. It is a home.'

He said the words with the warmth of love

and she smiled, remembering how forbidding her childhood home, an old nunnery, had looked from outside, yet how homelike it had been.

'It's the people inside that make a home,' she said, and saw his surprise.

Then his smile.

And something changed...

Something inside her gave way, weakening her when she would have liked to be strong.

Needed to be strong...

Tariq glanced at his companion, aware of the complications he was undoubtedly bringing into his life by insisting she stay in the palace. She would be accommodated in the women's house, which he knew, both from his early childhood within its confines and from sisters, aunts and cousins, was a hotbed of intrigue, gossip, innuendo and often scandal.

But if she was family this was where she belonged.

And if the Ta'wiz was genuine, and the thrill

he'd felt as he'd touched it suggested it was, then this was where it, too, belonged.

She was looking all around her, taking in the forbidding walls, a small frown teasing her delicate eyebrows.

'The gold on the walls?' she said. 'I took it to be decoration—a bit odd on a fortress but still.'

She paused and turned to look at him.

'But it's script, isn't it? That lovely flowing Arabic script? What does it say?'

He could lie—tell her anything—tell her it said 'Welcome', but the memory of his father's anger as he'd marched, often dragging his eight-year-old son, around the fortress walls, demanding the words be written faster, was imprinted in his mind.

As were the words!

He looked out at them now, as if to read them, although they were written on his heart.

'They say,' he explained slowly—reluctantly— "The head must rule the heart."'

'All the way round?' the visitor asked, obviously astonished.

Tariq shrugged.

'It is my father's motto and there may be variations on the theme,' he said, trying hard for casual while remembered anger tore at him. 'Here and there he may have put, "The heart must follow the head," but you get the gist of it.'

'And he wrote it all the way around?'

The woman, Lila, was wide-eyed in disbelief.

"And inside too,' Tariq told her, finally summoning up a small smile as the silliness of the whole thing struck him. 'He claimed it was an ancient ancestral ruling that had kept the tribe in power for so many generations. But in truth I think it was to annoy First Mother, who had the temerity to complain when he took a second wife.'

Ya lahwey, why was he telling this woman the story? Didn't the British have a saying about washing dirty linen in public? Wasn't that what he was doing?

But the pain he'd felt for his mother—First Mother—had imprinted that time like a fiery brand in his memory and still it burned when he remembered it.

Beside him he heard the visitor murmuring, and just made out the faintly spoken words— 'The head must rule the heart.'

'Maybe,' she finally said, loudly enough for him to hear, 'it is a good rule to live by. Do you follow it?'

You don't have to answer that, his ruling head told him, but as she'd asked...

'For my sins, I do,' he admitted, as they waited for the big gate to be opened. 'My head told me that the country needed doctors more than it needed more princes, and children's doctors in particular, to take health facilities to those who live far from the city.'

He paused.

He'd said enough.

But as the visitor gasped at the vision inside the palace walls—his father's vision—he felt compelled to finish what he'd been saying.

'It has caused a rift between us, my father and I.'

'I'm sorry,' she said softly, but then she looked

around and he had to smile at the astonishment on the woman's beautiful face. The old walls of the fort might remain, but inside was an earthly paradise made possible by the unlikely combination of oil and water. Oil revenue paid for all the water in his land, paid to have it desalinated from the ocean, so once what had been desert could blossom with astonishing beauty.

'But this is unbelievable,' the woman, Lila, whispered, turning her head this way and that as she took in the formal gardens, the bloom-covered bowers, the fountains and hedges, and carefully laid-out mosaic paths.

'It has been my father's life work,' Tariq told her, pride in his voice hiding the tug he felt in his heart as he thought of his father, ailing now, distanced from him, heart-sore over Khalil, a son from his second wife. Once he, Tariq, had chosen to do medicine Khalil had been brought up to be ruler, trained almost from birth. But now Khalil was ill with leukaemia his father was caught in a tussle over his choice of a successor should Khalil not survive.

Wanting Tariq to change his mind but too proud to beg...

Tariq shook away the exhaustion threatening to engulf him. He'd get his visitor settled, sleep for a few hours, then return to the hospital. He'd already assigned a staff member to act as guide and liaison for the new doctor but of course she was at the hospital, not here.

He'd get...he paused, his mind ranging through numerous sisters, half-sisters, female cousins and friends... Barirah.

Khalil's oldest half-sister, faithful and devoted like her name. Looking after Dr Halliday would take her mind off her brother's illness and her devastation that her own bone-marrow donation had failed to cure him.

The vehicle pulled up at the base of the shallow steps leading up to the covered loggia that surrounded the entire building. While the driver held the door for the newcomer, Tariq strode ahead, summoning a servant and sending her to find his half-sister.

Dr Halliday was following more slowly, turning as she came up each step to look back at the garden, as if fascinated by its extravagant beauty. On reaching the top, she glanced around at the array of shoes and sandals outside the front door, and he saw her smile as she slipped off the flat shoes she was wearing.

'It's like picture books I've seen,' she said, turning the smile towards him. 'All the shoes of different shapes and sizes, all the sandals, outside the door.'

It was only because he hadn't slept that her smile caught at something in his chest, and he was relieved when Barirah appeared, pausing by his side to kiss his cheek, asking about her brother, already knowing there'd be no new news.

'I need you to look after our guest,' he told her. 'She is coming to work at the hospital but I want her living here.'

Barirah raised her eyebrows, but Tariq found he couldn't explain.

'Come,' he said, leading her to the edge of the paved area where the newcomer still gazed at the garden. 'Dr Halliday, this is Barirah, my sister—'

'One of his many sisters and only a half one at that,' Barirah interrupted him. 'And I'm sure you have a better name than Dr Halliday.'

The visitor smiled, and held out her hand.

'I am Lila,' she said, her smile fading, turning to a slight frown, as she looked more closely at Barirah.

And seeing them together, Barirah now wearing an almost identical expression, Tariq cursed under his breath, blaming his tiredness for not realising the full extent of the complications that would arise—had arisen, in fact—by bringing Lila Halliday to the palace. Better by far that she'd stayed at the hospital where she'd just have been another doctor in a white coat, rather than possibly a first cousin to a whole host of family, not to mention niece to Second Mother.

And wasn't *that* going to open a can of worms!

'Who is she?' Barirah was demanding, moving from Lila to stand in front of Tariq, easing him back so she could speak privately.

'She might be your cousin,' was all Tariq could manage.

'Nalini's daughter? And you've brought her here? Are you mad? Can't you imagine how Second Mother's going to react to this? I might not remember much about that time but the tales of her reaction to Nalini's disappearance have become modern legends. Second Mother burnt her clothes on a pyre in the garden and our father had to build a fountain because nothing would grow where they had burnt.'

Tariq touched his half-sister's shoulder.

'Lila came looking for her family and I think that might be us,' he said gently. 'Isn't that enough reason for us to welcome her?'

Barirah rolled her eyes but turned back to look at the visitor, still standing at the edge of the loggia.

'You're right,' she said, and heaved a deep, deep sigh. 'She's family so she's welcome, but...'

She turned back to look at Tariq.

'You'd better be around to protect her. Don't you dare just dump her on me and expect me to run interference with Second Mother. I'm already a pariah in her eyes because I refuse to marry.'

Lila had guessed the conversation the Sheikh and the young woman who looked so like her had been about her, but what could she do?

Put on her shoes and leave the complex? Walk out through the beautiful gardens and the forbidding stone walls and—

Then what?

Besides, there was this nonsense about the Ta'wiz—about her mother being a thief.

Could she walk away from that?

Definitely not!

And being here in the palace, she might be able to find out what had happened way back then, learn things about her mother—and possibly her father too. And wasn't that why she'd come to Karuba?

She turned as the pair came towards her.

The woman called Barirah smiled at her.

'Tariq tells me we are probably cousins—that you are probably Nalini's daughter,' she said, in a softly modulated voice. 'So, as family, you are more than welcome.'

She hesitated then leaned forward and kissed Lila on both cheeks.

The gesture brought tears to Lila's eyes. Tiredness from the journey, she was sure, but Barirah must have seen them for she put her arms around Lila's shoulders and drew her into a hug.

'Come, I will find you a room and someone to look after you. Tariq, our guest might like some refreshment. She doesn't need to face the whole family at the moment, so perhaps you could order some lunch for the two of you in the arbour outside the green guest room? I have appointments I can't miss.'

Ignoring Tariq's protest that he needed to get back to the hospital, Barirah put her arm around Lila's shoulders to lead her into the house.

'I will put you in the green room—it was Nalini's room but has been redecorated. You might as well know now, because it's the first bit of gossip that you'll hear. My mother, who was Nalini's sister, went mad when Nalini left and destroyed the room and all the belongings she'd left behind. My mother is still bitter, but at least my brother's illness—he is battling leukaemia—is keeping her fully occupied at the moment.'

The flood of information rattled around in Lila's head. Jet-lag, she decided. She'd think about it all later.

Think about why the man walking down the marble hall behind them was sending shivers up her spine as well.

It had to be jet-lag…

'But it's beautiful!'

Having led her down innumerable corridors, Barirah had finally opened a very tall, heavy, wooden door to reveal what a first glance seemed like an underwater grotto of some kind.

The 'green' used to describe the room was as pale as the shallowest of water running up on a beach on a still day—translucent, barely there, yet as welcoming as nature itself. It manifested itself in the silk on the walls and the slightly darker tone in the soft curtains, held back by ropes of woven gold thread.

The bed stood four-square in the middle of the

room, the tall wooden posts holding a canopy of the same material as the curtains, while the bed-cover had delicate embroidery, vines and flowers picked out in gold and silver thread.

'It's unbelievable!' Lila whispered, walking across to a small chest of drawers to trace her fingers along the silver filigree design set into the wood. 'Is this design traditional?'

Barirah smiled.

'It is the most common motif in our decoration although by no means the only one. It shows the vine that grows over the dunes after rain, and see here...' delicate fingers traced the pattern '...the moonflower.'

It was the palest pink, perhaps more mauve in tone, open like a full moon, a half-open bud be-side it, and seeing it pain speared through Lila's heart and she fell to her knees, her hands reach-ing out to touch the flowers, to grasp the mate-rial and bring it to her face, feeling it against her skin, smelling it...

Barirah knelt beside her, held her, while she cried, then dried her eyes with a clean white tissue.

Lila turned to face her.

'My mother had a shawl—she wore it over her head and around her shoulders. It was this pattern! Why didn't I remember? How could I have forgotten that?'

Tariq, in the arbour outside the doors that opened into the garden, had heard the words, heard the anguish in the woman's voice, and wondered just how hard it must have been for a four-year-old to have lost not only her parents but the world as she had known it.

Barirah was helping Lila to her feet, comforting her with soft words and soothing noises, and he stepped back, showing the servants where to leave the food, then waiting for the two women to appear.

He sat, resting his tired eyes behind closed lids, dozed perhaps, aware he should be seeing his father, telling him of this development but not wanting to put further stresses on their guest.

Had he been less tired, he realised now—too late—he'd have taken her to the hospital, let her get on with her work. Officials could have confiscated the Ta'wiz, verified it, and it could have been returned to the palace, without her.

But even as these thoughts rambled through his exhausted brain, an image of the woman, Nalini's suspected daughter, hovered behind his eyelids, her dark almond eyes sparking with anger at him, her fingers clinging to the pendant—a last gift from her mother.

No way would she have given it up.

'He's been working far too hard.'

Barirah's voice woke him from the half-dream, woke him as his memories of Lila's angry eyes had shifted to an image of her soft lips—woke him just in time, really...

The two women joined him in the arbour, Barirah making her apologies for having to leave.

'But Tariq will take good care of you and, when you are rested, take you to the hospital to show you around.'

She gave Lila a brief kiss on the cheek and departed on silent feet, leaving Tariq to wonder again just how big a mistake he'd made in bringing the woman here.

His guest was eyeing the array of food with almost childlike delight.

'But what is it all? You must tell me,' she said, moving around the table to see each dish more clearly. 'Olives I know, although the pink ones are different. And the little white balls—cheeses? Hallie, my foster mother, made *labneh*—cheese from yoghurt—but it was a little dull.'

But there was tension beneath the flow of words, and Tariq realised that the young woman had been hit by so much information and so many new and emotional experiences in the few hours since she'd arrived that she was running on adrenalin.

'Sit,' he ordered, and tired as he was he stood up, selected a brightly patterned plate and began to place an array of small delicacies on it.

He handed it to her, laid a napkin on her knee and said, 'Try a little of each. You'll soon learn what you like and what you don't. And I'm sure you'll recognise tastes you're familiar with, though they may be delivered differently.'

She took the plate from him and looked up into his face.

'Thank you,' she said quietly, simply, her dark eyes smiling now, the lips he'd seen behind his eyelids curving slightly.

He *definitely* should have taken her to the apartment at the hospital!

CHAPTER THREE

LILA WATCHED HER HOST, pouring cool lemon drinks into tall glasses.

'Can you tell me about my mother?' she asked, when he finally settled back in a fat-cushioned cane chair. 'Well, about Nalini, who might be my mother?'

He hesitated, tipped his head to one side as if the question might be better seen from another angle, then finally replied, 'What would you like to know?'

'What would I like to know?' she demanded. 'Everything, of course.'

He smiled.

'Tall order for over lunch,' he said, still obviously hesitant.

'Well, anything at all,' Lila suggested. 'What

made you think I was related to her? Something must have, as you said her name.'

Another smile, small but there—a reminiscent smile...

'You are very like her, not only in looks but in some of your mannerisms, or movements, something I cannot explain, although I could see it when I looked at you.'

Lila felt the words drop into the empty space inside her. They didn't fill the space, of course, but it did feel a little less empty.

'But who was she?' And why do you think she stole the Ta'wiz?'

No smile this time.

'Nalini was my father's second wife's sister, if you can follow that. To make it more complicated, in Karuba we talk about the wives as mothers, so my mother—my father's first wife— is First Mother, while Nalini's sister is Second Mother. Nalini was the younger sister and she came to live in the palace as Second Mother's companion. And, truthfully, when she arrived it was if a light had been switched on, and all the old shadows in the palace disappeared, bringing the place back to life because she was such fun.'

He paused and Lila knew he was back in that time, seeing pictures in his head.

'We loved her, all of us,' he added simply.

'So why would she leave? And why would you think her a thief?'

He shrugged.

'I was a child so I cannot answer that for you. You must realise that the theft—and Nalini's link to it—brought shame to Second Mother and she never forgave her sister for that. You will hear many stories and not all of them will be good ones, so you will have to sift them through for yourself. One of them, perhaps it was true, was that my father had arranged a marriage for her and she didn't wish to marry whoever it was—didn't want to be forced into an arranged marriage. This would have angered my father, and infuriated Second Mother, who was jealous of her sister's popularity and would have been pleased to see her go. But I can tell you that Nalini was beautiful, and she brought joy to many people.'

Again that hesitation, then he added, 'I was eight, and I loved her.'

Lila closed her eyes, trying to picture her mother—to picture the man beside her as a child. She tucked the words 'beautiful' and 'joy' into the empty space and accepted that she'd hear little more from this man now.

Some other time she'd ask again, but in the meantime, living here in what he'd called the women's house, she did not doubt she'd hear the other stories he'd spoken of.

Not all of them would be good, he'd also said, but maybe they would help her put together a picture of the woman who'd become her mother.

In the meantime…

Should she ask?

But how else to find out?

'And my father?'

He shook his head, as if sorry this conversation had begun. Not that a headshake was going to stop her.

She waited, her eyes on his face. He'd taken off his headscarf before meeting them in the arbour, and without it casting shadows on his face she could see the lines of weariness.

But doctors often looked like that...

'We really don't know,' he admitted. 'There was a lot of talk—speculation—but there was also the fact that she might have gone away on her own. No one knew.'

He bowed his head, as if suddenly overwhelmed by exhaustion.

'I need to sleep,' he said. 'It was a long night.'

'Is there a problem at the hospital?' she asked. 'When we video chatted, you seemed so positive. You sounded excited that things going well enough for you to begin the outreach programme you want to run.'

Dark eyes met hers—not dark dark, but with a greenish tinge, and framed by eyelashes most women would die for.

'The hospital *is* working well, the outreach programme ready to begin, but...'

He looked so shattered it was all she could do not to reach out and touch him—to offer comfort.

'It is my brother,' he explained, his voice deepened by despair. 'He's been battling leukaemia for four years and just when we think it's gone for good, he comes out of remission. He has had an autologous stem cell transplant and an allogenic one from me, and some other close members of his family, but there's a kink...'

He paused then added, 'There's a kink—that's a very unprofessional explanation but it's how I think of it—just some slight difference in a chromosome that makes the sibling matches not quite right. I've been searching worldwide donor bases to see if I can find a match.'

Leukaemia, she knew, came in so many forms, so many sub-types and deviations and, as Tariq had said, there were many chromosomal differences that made both treatment and likely outcomes very difficult to predict.

'How old is he?' she asked, thinking that the younger a child was diagnosed, the more chance he had.

'Eighteen now. He has been ill for three years— well, ill, then in remission, then ill again. You must know how it goes.'

Tariq's voice told her of his despair and she knew he understood just how little chance his brother had of a full recovery.

Of any recovery?

'But Khalil is a fighter,' he added, 'and we're all fighting with him. You'll get to meet him at the hospital, of course, although probably only through glass as his immune system is wrecked.'

Lila shook her head, aware of the stress and agony this must be causing his family.

But what could she say?

Then Tariq was speaking again, so she didn't have to say anything.

'You should rest now and I definitely need sleep,' he said. 'But perhaps, by five, you might be sufficiently rested to visit the hospital. I had planned tomorrow to be an orientation day for you—more learning your way around than work—but this afternoon the unit I ordered for the outreach clinic will be delivered and as you'll be using it quite a lot, you might like to join me when I take possession of it?'

'I'd love to,' Lila told him with genuine enthusiasm, because it had been his description of the service he hoped to provide to the children of nomadic tribes that had heightened her interest in Karuba—that had given her more reason to come than just the search for her family.

'Shall we say five at the main entrance to the women's quarters?' he said, standing up and moving to ease kinks of what must be tiredness from his limbs.

'If I can ever find the main entrance again,' Lila said with a smile.

It was just a smile—nothing more—Tariq told himself as he strode away as swiftly as his tired limbs would carry him.

But the smile had touched some part of him that rarely recognised emotion.

Surely not his heart!

No, he believed his father was right—their people had survived for generations in a dangerous, arid land because the head ruled the heart, making decisions based on practicality, sound business principles and common sense, rather than emotion.

Worry over Khalil was confusing him, and seeing Nalini again—well, Nalini's daughter—remembering that bitter time in the palace when even the children had been affected by the poisonous atmosphere—anyone would be confused.

Barirah was right, he shouldn't have brought her here.

But the Ta'wiz!

With Khalil so ill…

His head could scoff all it liked but some ancient instinct, not necessarily in his heart but something deep in his soul, told him the Ta-wiz should be here in the palace…

He made his way slowly through the gardens towards his own quarters. He needed sleep more than anything—just a few hours—but as he reached the small courtyard in front of his wing of the palace, he saw again his father's words, this time rendered in the mosaic tiles in the courtyard.

He should speak to his mother, tell her of Lila

Halliday's arrival, even though gossip about it would surely have reached her by now.

All the more reason to talk to her personally, he told himself. But weariness overcame duty and he walked up the shallow steps and shuffled off his shoes, heading into the house to the sanctuary of his bedroom.

He would sleep, and later, when he met the doctor, he would set aside the confusion of this morning and meet her as a colleague, a colleague he hoped would help him fulfil a dream he'd held for a long time.

To bring better health to the children outside the cities and towns—to ensure they were inoculated against the worst of childhood diseases—because he knew the divide between the towns and the desert was diminishing, and the children of the nomads were part of the future of his country. Health and education—with these two platforms, they could become anything they wished…

He slept…

* * *

Lila woke with a start to find a young woman sitting on a mat by her door, her hands busy, fingers flying as she did some delicate needlework.

'I am Sousa,' she said, rising gracefully to her feet. 'I am here to look after you. You would like refreshment? A cool drink? Tea, perhaps? I know English people like tea, but I don't know very much about Australians.'

She was so openly curious Lila had to smile.

'Australians drink a lot of tea,' she said, not adding that many of them drank a lot of beer and wine as well. Her family hadn't, though not for any apparent reason, happy to accept a glass of wine to toast a special occasion but not bothering otherwise.

But thinking of her family—the one that was real to her—reminded her that she was here on a mission, a double mission now, not only to find out all she could about her parents but also to clear her mother's name.

And Sousa might at least know something!

'I'd love some tea,' she said. 'Perhaps you could

join me and explain a little about how things work at the palace. I am to meet my boss—Sheikh al Askeba—at five, but that still gives us time for a chat.'

Sousa disappeared with an alacrity that suggested she was dying to find out more about the foreign visitor, returning with a tea tray only minutes later, complete with warm scones wrapped in a table napkin, and jam and cream to go on them.

'Sheikh al Askeba—that's Tariq, your boss—he should be Crown Prince because he's the oldest son, but he wanted to study and fought with his father for the right to be a doctor, which is very good for our country as he has built the hospital, and brought in many famous medical people from overseas, but that meant Khalil had to be Crown Prince and now he is so ill, everyone is worried. If he dies, who will the King choose as his successor?'

'Are there only the two sons? And can daughters not take over?'

Sousa looked horrified at the second idea.

'Daughters are women,' she said, making Lila smile. Talk about stating the obvious! 'The King, he has many daughters, and maybe one of their husbands could take over as the country's ruler because most of the daughters are married to other members of the royal family.'

'Is it a worry?' Lila asked. 'Does it matter who takes over as long as he's a good ruler?'

Sousa's eyes widened with might have been horror.

'Of course it matters,' she said. 'Whoever takes over—the crown will pass down through their line of the family, and the old king's line will lose... I do not know the word. It is more than power, it is to do with presence.'

'Lose face?' Lila suggested, and Sousa nodded.

Great, Lila thought. *Not only am I here as the daughter of a thief, but it seems I've stepped into the middle of some complicated family intrigue.*

But she'd take the King's words as advice and let her head rule her heart, do her job, find out all she could about her parents, then go happily back to Australia to get on with her life—a life she'd put on hold for far too long already.

She finished her tea, only half listening to Sousa's chat as she dressed in another conservative outfit ready for her visit to the hospital.

With Sheikh Tariq al Askeba...

No, with her colleague and her boss.

Head—remember, use your head.

Besides, she was reasonably certain she'd only been attracted to him because he'd seemed so exhausted, and having felt that way herself many times during her career, it had been fellow feeling for a colleague, nothing more.

Sousa led her to the front door, where one of the big black cars was already waiting, Tariq standing outside, chatting to the driver.

'Right on time,' he said to her, glancing at his watch, then smiling at her.

Whoosh! All composure fled. Where *was* her head? One smile and she went weak at the knees.

Jet-lag, she reminded herself. It must be jet-lag!

'Good afternoon,' she said brightly, possibly too brightly, because she'd realised that if he'd been impressive in his regal outfit, he was just as impressive in what were obviously 'work' clothes. Pale fawn chinos that clung to his hips and showed a shapely butt and strong legs, and a pale blue denim shirt that for some reason made his eyes seem greener.

And she was noticing?

She didn't do noticing men—well, not much anyway—too busy with study, then work, and the continual search for her identity. There'd been boyfriends from time to time, but no one serious, and she suspected it was a psychological block to do with her identity, or lack of one…

But this man drew notice like no one else ever had.

Was it the aura of power he had?

The power she'd experienced as he'd swept into her life, claimed her as family, and insisted she stay at the palace…

She climbed into the car, determined to be professional, asking about the mobile clinic he'd set up. Had he seen the specially designed unit?

He'd still been awaiting its delivery when they'd spoken.

But while her questions had been polite professionalism, his responses surprised her, for his passion for the project echoed like warm treacle in his voice, and she found her own excitement building.

'Our first trip will be to the mountains,' he was saying. 'They are on the very border of Karuba, and for thousands of years have been the location for the summer camp of the largest nomad tribe. Years ago they hunted the leopard there, but today many of the same tribespeople work in conservation, for the Arabian leopard came close to extinction.'

'I didn't realise there was such a thing,' Lila said. A tiny thread of memory sparked something in her brain. She tried to catch it, but it was gone.

'Our leopard is smaller, and paler than leopards in other countries, almost sand coloured between its spots, but it is still a beautiful animal.'

Lila heard again the passion in his voice and

knew this was a man who not only loved his country, but would dedicate himself to it.

So much for his head ruling his heart!

She looked out the window to see that the car was entering yet another walled garden, this one with a new, modern building rising up in the centre of it.

'The hospital?'

He nodded.

'Do you want to see your brother before you show me around?' she asked, and knew it had been the right question when his lips twitched in what might almost have been a smile.

'I would if it won't inconvenience you too much.'

'No worries,' she said. 'Anyway, I'd like to meet him, even if it's only through glass.'

No reaction.

She glanced towards him and wondered if his silence was telling her she wouldn't be welcome—though why that would be, she couldn't say.

The car drew up at a small side entrance.

A private entrance?

Royal privilege?

But the group of people coming out, men and women, dressed much as she and Tariq were, suggested it was for staff. One or two of them greeted him, one of the women stopping to talk for a few minutes. Unsure of herself now, Lila waited by the car, until her host, apparently forgetting she was with him, strode inside, appearing a few seconds later and looking relieved when he realised she was following.

'I'm sorry, I was distracted. Khalil's mother, Second Mother, might have been with him. But I've been told she's resting in a nearby room.'

He hesitated.

'This is awkward for you?' Lila guessed. 'I can wait in the car, or anywhere really.'

To her surprise, Tariq smiled, and she realised it was the first spontaneous smile she'd seen, others having been nothing more than a twitch of his lips or efforts at politeness, strained efforts at that.

It was a smile that lit up his face, and sparkled in his eyes, doing strange things deep inside Lila's chest.

Lungs, not heart, she told herself, and smiled back.

'Less awkward now,' he said, 'but, as I said, Second Mother blamed Nalini for many things.'

He paused, before amending the words to, 'Most things, including, I'm sure, the fact that she had more daughters than sons.'

The smile still twitched at his lips, but disappeared when he said, 'She could well be unkind to you. To her, within the hospital you will be staff so accorded no more attention than she gives to our servants—which is very little—but at the palace, remember you are my guest. You do not need to put up with rudeness from her.'

'Well, that sounds like heaps of fun,' Lila told him, hoping to see the smile again. 'I can't wait.'

But his eyes were sombre when he said, 'I'm sorry—talking of Second Mother this way—but she is a deeply unhappy woman.'

'Her son has been battling death for three years—it must have put great pressure on her.'

'Ha, you are like Nalini,' he replied. 'Seeing the good in everyone. Even at eight I remember that of her. She reprimanded me for teasing my sisters, telling me that just because I was born a boy it didn't make me better than them.'

Again the smile and that little flip in Lila's chest.

'Though of course I was—everyone knew that—and all the servants treated me accordingly. Wrong in this day of political correctness, but it's how things were—the son was the Little Prince; the daughters were currency to be traded for wealth or ambition.'

'And my mother didn't like that?'

'Not one little bit! In fact, she encouraged my sisters to tease me, and probably helped make a better person of me as a result.'

This time Lila's reaction was a bloom of warmth, definitely in her heart.

Tariq had given her another scrap of the picture she would build of her mother, to be carefully stored until she had a whole.

Tariq was talking now of families whilst leading her along corridors he obviously knew well. So it was as family Lila stood outside the glass observation window and looked in at the pale, emaciated young man, his skin as pale as the sheets he lay on.

He could be my cousin, she thought, then turned to Tariq, who was discussing the patient's progress with a nurse.

Could be?

There was one way she could find out for sure.

'You could test me,' she said, then realised she'd interrupted. 'Oh, I'm sorry, but it just occurred to me and seemed to make sense. We're not siblings but perhaps, if I am related, I have the "kink" you spoke of—the slight chromosomal difference. Many bone-marrow donors aren't close relatives—that's why we have the worldwide donor register.'

Tariq and the nurse were both staring at her.

'Don't you see?' she insisted. 'It's worth a try!'

'But we're not here for this. I want to show you the mobile clinic.'

Tariq was obviously thrown by her suggestion, but Lila wasn't about to give in.

'I can see that anytime,' she told him. 'Well, later, but you must have a pathology department, let's test me now. Consider for a moment that Nalini really is my mother—you're the one who saw the resemblance and took me to the palace as family. If that's the case, then I'm related to Khalil. And if I'm compatible enough to help, isn't it better to know sooner rather than later?'

The nurse was speaking now, apparently urging Tariq to go along with the idea, although she was speaking in the local language so Lila was just guessing.

'You know what's involved if you are compatible?' Tariq asked, and Lila smiled.

'More or less, but right now that's not important. If I'm not a good match it's not an issue.'

He frowned at her.

'Are you always this impulsive?' he demanded, and Lila had to laugh.

'Ask my family,' she said. 'They will all tell you I am the most cautious, careful, planning kind of person they have ever known. I've been teased about it all my life, but this is right, I can feel it. Please, Tariq, what harm can it possibly do?'

Tariq stared at her, taken aback by how beautiful she was when she laughed, mesmerised by the glint in her eyes and the lingering smile on her face.

She'd swept into his life that morning and he'd met her with anger in his heart because she had come to his country wearing something precious to his people—something stolen long ago.

Then he'd seen Nalini in her and been thrust back to his childhood, and his confusion—aided by exhaustion—had grown from there.

And now she was insisting on a blood test so she could offer herself as a donor to a cousin she'd never met?

A 'maybe' cousin...

Of course it was unlikely she'd be compatible—the chances possibly as high as a million to one. Although as a reasonably close relative, if she *was* a reasonably close relative...

'Come with me,' he said.

Not that she seemed to mind. She pressed her fingers to the glass of the observation window as if taking farewell of Khalil, then fell in beside Tariq as he strode down the corridor. Her head bobbed about level with his shoulder and she took three steps to his two, but she kept up with him, as if accepting some unspoken challenge.

A pathology nurse, alerted by Khalil's nurse, was waiting in a nearby blood collection room.

'Do you want blood or a cheek swab?' Lila asked him as they entered.

'I think blood,' he said, resigned now to the test and thinking ahead to being able to check other things from the blood.

'Makes sense,' Lila told him, greeting the nurse with a warm smile and settling into the chair. 'You can get the HLA match from either but if you've got blood you can check for any infection I might have.'

Tariq thought of the HLA—human leukocyte antigen—a protein on the surface of white blood cells that needed to be matched to the recipient's. His own had been nowhere near a close enough match, and back when Khalil had first been diagnosed that had been devastating. Tariq couldn't help but feel responsible for the young half-brother who would rule the country because *he* had chosen a different path.

You were following your head, not your heart, he reminded himself, and glanced towards the woman whose sudden appearance in his life was causing so much disruption. The nurse was sticking a plaster over the tiny pinprick on the inside of her elbow.

'See, it took no time at all,' Lila said, smiling at him. 'So now you can show me our mobile clinic.'

He explained to the nurse about the tests he wanted done, then escorted his new colleague along a corridor towards the back of the building.

'It's a good thing there are signs here in English,' she said, 'or I'd need a guide like Sousa to show me around the hospital.'

He glanced at her, wondering if she was as carefree as she sounded. Or was she covering tumultuous emotion with light chatter? It seemed to him she must be, given all that had happened to her since her arrival in Karuba less than twelve hours ago.

He'd have liked to ask, and, realising that, he had to wonder why.

Did it matter what she was feeling?

And on considering that question, he rather thought it did—which was a conclusion as surprising as the discovery that his new employee had arrived in the country wearing the Ta'wiz.

CHAPTER FOUR

LILA FOLLOWED TARIQ out of yet another door. If left on her own she'd never find her way out of the hospital, let alone back to the palace!

He strode across a courtyard to a large garage, pressing numbers into a key pad and watching a long door slide open.

Inside, painted dark blue and gold, stood a pristinely new prime mover with two trailers attached.

'Oh, it's a B-Double! What a beauty!' Lila exclaimed, heading around to the driver's side and hoisting herself up to open the door and look inside.

Only it wasn't the driver's door but the passenger's.

'Oh—of course—you drive on the wrong side of the road over here.'

She yelled the words from her perch high above Tariq, then clambered across the two beautifully constructed seats to look at the controls.

'We're supposed to be looking at the clinic *in* the trailers,' Tariq said, though there wasn't much conviction in his voice, as if her actions had bemused him.

'Oh, but I just have to check this out first,' Lila told him. 'It's fantastic and from the look of it will take you anywhere. Was it built here or did you have to import it?'

'Germany.'

The answer was brief enough for Lila to realise maybe she was overdoing her delight.

Never mind, she'd check out the prime mover some other time, preferably when Tariq wasn't around.

She clambered back over the seats, climbed down the first steps, and leapt lightly to the ground.

'Pop, my foster father, drove big rigs,' she explained, then fell in beside him once again as he led the way to the lead semi-trailer, slightly smaller than the second.

'I've had this set up as a mobile theatre. Although the primary purpose of the mobile clinic will be paediatric, there are always adults who need attention, often quite urgently, so it made sense to be prepared for anything. It's very basic, for minor surgery only, and as all the mobile clinic doctors have had anaesthetic training, the second doctor can always step in as anaesthetist if required.'

He used a key pad again to open the door and Lila peered in at what looked like a very small but beautifully appointed emergency department. A few chairs to wait at, a desk taking minimal space, two curtained-off areas that would be treatment rooms, and a closed door at the end— the operating theatre?

'Did you design it?" she asked, turning to Tariq and reading satisfaction on his face as he looked around.

'Bit by bit, and slowly but surely, with a lot of input from other medical staff. We will carry everything we need, even down to blood and plasma supplies, oxygen, anaesthetic, surgical tools, gowns, gloves—the lot.'

'It's amazing,' Lila told him, and was pleased when he smiled.

'But wait until you see the second part,' he said, leading the way out of the unit and relocking the door.

'Oh, but it's fantastic!' He had opened the door on the larger trailer and she gazed around in awe at the paintings of animals and birds on the walls of the unit, feeling the smoothness of the floor that had been made to look like sand.

'The animals and birds, are they local species?' she asked, and was shown the peregrine falcon, the leopard, a little rabbit-like creature Tariq told her was a cape hare.

'And that's a gazelle, isn't it?' Lila asked, pointing to a shy-looking animal peering around a curtained cubicle.

'It is indeed. You'll learn the rest in time. The children will educate you because they have grown up with these creatures.'

'Even the fox?' Lila asked, pointing with delight at a cheeky red fox digging its way out from behind a cupboard.

One corner was fenced off with soft carpet and toys, while bookshelves held bright picture books. Even the curtains of the treatment rooms were decorated with pictures of the desert dunes, and the mountains Lila had seen as the plane came in, while a friendly camel seemed to loom over a cabinet.

'It's very special,' she said, and saw the pride on Tariq's face.

'It will be your domain, you know, although I will do the first trip with you, to introduce you to the chiefs and make arrangements with them for your accommodation. The second doctor on other trips will treat adult patients, and work with you when you need him or her. You'll also have a nurse, Rani, and an aide who doubles as administrator, Sybilla, on your team, and a—I don't know how to describe him—a guide who will oversee the operation. He will be accommodated with the driver, but it is he who will be your protection at all times.'

'Protection?' Lila queried.

'Not from the tribespeople but from trouble. He will handle things like the timetable, sort out delays, and generally make life run smoothly for you and your staff.'

'He sounds like a great guy,' Lila said, 'not to mention useful.'

'He is,' came the reply, but it was less definite than Lila had expected. In fact, the words kind of fizzled out as if in saying it Tariq had been struck by some other thought.

Lila poked around inside what she realised now was a converted shipping container. What fun this would be—and what a great chance to see the country of her mother—if Nalini *was* her mother—the place she'd sought in her dreams for so long.

As Tariq stepped outside, he thought about how testing for bone-marrow compatibility included a DNA test—but it was strictly confidential.

Maybe later she might like to know—ask about DNA testing as confirmation of who she was…

Did it matter?

He had no idea, he only knew that if he'd been thrown into complete turmoil by the arrival of his newest hospital recruit, how in heaven's name must she be feeling?

Lost?

Bewildered?

Overpowered by too much information too soon?

He glanced at her, and saw that the honey colour had faded from her skin, and small lines had appeared on her cheeks.

'You're exhausted,' he said, more roughly than he'd intended. 'Come, we will return to the palace and you can sleep. There is no need for you to work tomorrow either. This must have been a tumultuous day for you.'

She offered him a tired smile that, if his heart had had any say in it, might have felt a tweak, but with his head in charge it did little more than anger him for pushing on when obviously the visit to the mobile clinic had proved too much for her.

'This way,' he said. 'I'll take you home.'

'Home?' she asked, with a better smile this time.

And this time his head lost the battle…

They drove back to the palace in comparative silence, Lila pointing out the way the moon laid a silver path across the water towards the city, Tariq telling her that the dunes by moonlight were even more beautiful.

'I want to see them, I want to see it all,' Lila told him. 'And the flamingo lake the steward on the plane told me about and—'

She stopped abruptly.

'I want to ask you something but I'm afraid it will sound silly,' she said.

'I doubt if anything would sound silly after what we've discovered today,' Tariq told her, and was rewarded with another smile.

'It's about sand,' she said. 'The box my mother had, the box I keep remembering, had sand in it and I'm sure the sand was pink. She would put a little of it into the Ta'wiz, but only a little, and very carefully, as if the pink sand was precious and she couldn't afford to spill it.'

Now Tariq felt his heart at work for a different reason. That Nalini—it *had* to have been Nalini—having left her land, had kept the sacred sand that meant so much to all his people. Not only kept it but guarded it jealously.

Lila was waiting for an answer, but he wasn't sure he could speak through the emotion in his throat.

He took a deep breath, told his head to take control, and explained. 'There *is* pink sand, in just one place in Karuba—a special place. The legend of it goes back through many, many generations of our people to the founding father, who was born on the sand near the flamingo lake. It was a long time ago—a time when many women died in childbirth, as did his mother. The story says she bled to death and the sand turned pink with blood, stayed that way ever since. People leaving the country take some of the pink sand with them. It is their connection to their land, almost like a promise to return.'

There, he'd said it, but when he glanced towards his companion to see her reaction, he saw her shoulders shake and tears running from her eyes.

Moved beyond measure, he reached out and drew her close, nestling her slight body against his, murmuring soothing words, unconsciously returning to his native tongue.

But surely that's how her parents would have soothed her, he thought, leaning over slightly to breathe in the slightly lemon tang of her hair.

He felt her body settling, then stiffen as she tried to ease away.

'I'm okay now,' she said, the words muffled as she wiped at her tears. 'It was the thought of my mother taking it as a promise to return. A promise she couldn't keep.'

'Some things are beyond our control,' he told her, his heart definitely affected by the words.

'I know, and at least now I know why it meant so much to her. I've always remembered the pink sand, you see, and for so long I thought I must have imagined it. In my mind I can see it, but whenever I looked up countries with pink sand, nothing was ever right.'

'Well, now you know,' he said gently as the car entered the palace gates.

'Thank you,' she said, and as the car slid to a stop at the main entrance, she opened the door and slipped out, whispering a quiet goodnight.

Tariq waited long enough to ensure Sousa was at the door, waiting for Lila, before asking the driver to drop him at his quarters.

What must have been the longest day on record was finally coming to an end...

Lila slipped off her shoes outside the door, and felt the last remnants of energy from what had been a very long and eventful day drain from her.

'Come,' Sousa told her, taking her by the elbow and leading her into the house. 'I have a small meal ready for you, then a bath and straight into bed. You have done too much on your first day in the country.'

Done too much and found out too much! Lila realised. And it was the 'finding out' part that was causing her most concern. Yes, she had a name for her mother, all the pieces slotting into place, making her more sure than ever that Nalini—Tariq's Nalini—was her mother. But where did the theft fit in? Why would her mother have been so desperate to leave the place she'd clearly loved that she would have stolen what were obviously precious treasures?

Especially when she intended to return—didn't the sand tell her that?

She stood at the doorway leading out into the courtyard, and looked at the beautiful garden, turned to a fairy wonderland by the moonlight and probably some discreet lighting.

Had her mother stood here?

Thinking of what?

A man?

A man she loved?

Dreaming impossible dreams of them being together?

A night bird called somewhere in the garden, another answering it.

Lovers?

Sleep had come easily, but some inner clock had Lila up at dawn. Dressing swiftly, she went out into the garden, wandering along the paths, pausing to admire a beautiful topiary peacock, its tail spread in front of a sculpted, leafy female.

Small hedges divided the garden into rooms, sometimes with a reflection pool or a fountain at the centre, and off to one side slightly higher hedges formed a labyrinth. She danced along its paths with delight.

'I understood the idea was to follow the path in quiet contemplation,' a voice said, and she turned to see Tariq outside the outer hedge.

'Only until you get into the centre,' she told him. 'Then you ask your question or make a wish—well, that's what we believed as children when we drew labyrinths in the sand at the beach.'

'And did you ask a question or make a wish?'

Tariq asked, intrigued by the thought that the hedge pattern had a deeper meaning. For Lila, at any rate.

'I asked a question,' she told him.

'And the answer made you skip all the way back?'

He sounded so cynical she had to laugh.

'Of course it did. I asked if I'd done the right thing in coming to Karuba and in my heart I knew immediately that I had.' She paused, then added, 'And in my head as well,' nodding towards the bits of golden script that could be glimpsed through the foliage on the outer walls.

To her surprise he gave a little huff of laughter, and Lila had to curb the urge to dance and skip some more.

Head, she reminded herself.

'So,' she said, 'when do we set off on our first big adventure? Can we go today?'

'I would have thought that a day like yesterday would have left you exhausted. In fact, I know you were exhausted last night.'

She smiled breezily at him.

'But that was before I had a really good sleep and a walk in the labyrinth.'

He didn't need to say anything, his face telling her he didn't believe a word she was saying.

'I really did sleep well,' she said, 'and the test results will take, what? Two or three weeks for detailed analysis? Shouldn't we be using the time to go out to the nomad camp while the tribespeople are still in the mountains? I imagine they don't stay in one place for very long, wherever they are.'

Tariq studied the slight figure, still half-hidden behind a hedge, today dressed in a pale colour that reminded him of the butter made from camel milk.

Was it cream?

He let his head run with questions for a few seconds mainly so it could regain a little control over whatever it was in his chest that kept reacting to this woman.

'Actually, the clinic unit left this morning. I had intended flying out tomorrow but I can do the first visit on my own—well, with the nurse and administrator. Just to see how it all works—find out what doesn't work, or what could be improved.'

'So, we can both go tomorrow? If it's to be my clinic then I'm the one who should be testing it, surely.'

His head would probably have found a good argument against this idea if she hadn't smiled when she'd said 'surely'.

And not just any smile, but a kind of teasing smile, as if daring him to argue.

Which, of course, he should.

'You may not feel quite so fit tomorrow—jet-lag can take time to grab hold of you.'

It was not a perfect argument—in fact, it was a very weak argument—but she'd emerged from behind the hedge and he realised she was barefoot—small slim feet with pale pink toenails glistening with dew, a few tiny shreds of grass clinging to her just visible ankles.

From his mother's love of Jane Austen and Regency romances, he knew women's ankles had been considered too erotic to be left uncovered and even in his own culture they were rarely seen.

It had bemused him in the past. During his postgraduate years in England women's ankles had been on show everywhere, and he'd wondered how they'd ever come to be considered a temptation.

But a fine strip of grass on a pale ankle was doing things to his body that had nothing to do with his head or his heart.

'Are you looking at my feet? Should I not be out here barefoot? Do you have a list of rules? I don't want to be offending anyone, even unintentionally.'

'Your feet are fine,' he managed, dragging his mind from images of other bits of grass on other parts of her body. 'Would you like Sousa to accompany you into the city today? Is there anything special you'd like to do?'

Resisting the urge to check if her feet had suddenly turned into claws, or maybe become webbed like a duck's, Lila looked into his eyes and shook her head.

'I think if I start work tomorrow today would best be spent getting to know my way around this place and learning its routines. I'll have to do some washing sometime, and then there are meals—I don't want Sousa to have to keep bringing meals to my room when obviously there's somewhere that other people eat.'

'I should have thought of that,' he said, looking concerned, although it was a very small matter. 'If Barirah is free today, she will show you around and introduce you to whatever family is living here at the moment. Otherwise Sousa will do it, and she will also organise your laundry. I apologise for pushing you into a strange environment without making sure you are comfortable in it.'

Lila laughed.

'I'm in a room that's like a mermaid's grotto, I have a woman who sits by my door awaiting orders, I have this beautiful garden to explore—I'm not exactly uncomfortable.'

Was it her laughter or the words that won a very small smile from her boss?

Whatever it was, she discovered that even a small smile was something not to be missed, lighting up his rather stern face and crinkling the skin at the corners of his eyes.

Her fingers tingled and she clenched her fists to fight the reaction. Of course she didn't want to touch those little wrinkles!

But danger lurked in this man in the form of an attraction that was new to her.

An attraction she had no idea how to handle…

Sousa's arrival to tell her breakfast was in the arbour broke up the meeting, which was just as well, from Lila's point of view.

'I'll talk to Barirah and get back to you,' Tariq said, but he didn't turn and walk away, while she, too, hesitated…

It's just being in a strange place—so many new experiences crowding in on her, Lila decided. No wonder she was confused.

She followed Sousa back to the arbour, and breakfasted on yoghurt and fruit and delicious rolls filled with soft cheese and dipped in honey, then lay back against soft cushions, replete.

'Are you asleep?'

Barirah was there, smiling down at her.

'Waking dreams,' Lila told her, not mentioning that walking through every one of them had been a tall, rather stern-looking sheikh. 'It's all so unbelievable, like stepping into a fairy tale.'

'There's a phrase I heard in America when I was studying there,' Barirah said. 'You ain't seen nothin' yet!'

Lila laughed.

'I've seen enough to know that's probably very true. So where do we start? Maybe at the front door—the door I've been coming in and out of—and go from there so I get to know my way to my room and back without making a faux pas. I was in the garden without my shoes this morning, and Tariq looked most disapproving. Do you not go barefoot outside? Feel the dew on the grass, the sand between your toes?'

'Of course we go barefoot inside all the time, and outside, too, when we wish,' Barirah assured her. 'Especially to feel the sand between our toes, but that's mostly at the beach. In the desert, we wear our sandals—I suppose because of scorpions.'

'Well, I'm glad you've told me that,' Lila said, although she was thinking of the strange expression on Tariq's face as he'd looked at her bare feet.

He must have been thinking s*omething*...

Barirah waited while Lila washed her face and hands and tidied her hair, before leading her to the front door, down a corridor that was becoming familiar, mainly because it was lined with portraits of women, some in the local dress, others looking at if they were going to a very fancy ball.

'It's the First Mothers' corridor, Barirah explained. 'These are portraits of all the first mothers who've lived in the palace since it was built.'

'And is there a Second Mothers' corridor?' Lila asked, and Barirah laughed.

'Of course, and even a Third Mothers' and a Fourth Mothers' but they are smaller, minor passageways in the building.'

Lila was intrigued.

'As befits their status?'

Another laugh.

'Not really. Some Second, Third or Fourth Mothers became the reigning king's favourites, so there are portraits of them in other rooms as well.'

'And this king's First Mother?'

'You want to see if that's where Tariq gets his stern looks?' Barirah teased. 'I'd have thought you'd have been more interested in the Second Mother—your aunt.'

'We can look at both,' Lila suggested, but something about Tariq's behaviour at the hospital—ensuring Second Mother wasn't with her son when they visited—made her wary of meeting the woman, for all that she was probably Lila's closest living relation.

First Mother looked suitably regal, and haughty enough for Lila to see Tariq in her features. She wore a purple shawl, embroidered with gold thread, over her head and shoulders, and stared down at those passing along the corridor with a certain manner of disdain. But the dark eyes—like Tariq's with a hint of green in them—looked kind.

But in the next corridor, it was Second Mother who looked every inch a queen, clad in a scarlet ballgown, diamonds dripping from her neck, arms and fingers, a tiara of them on her upswept dark hair.

'You don't look very much like her,' Lila said, turning from the portrait to her new friend.

Barirah smiled.

'I'm not at all, not in any way. I always tell people I'm from Tariq's side of the family and I suspect my mother does too. I'm okay to look at, but she was and still is a great beauty and most of my sisters are as well.'

'Yet you and I are alike—we saw that from the start,' Lila reminded her.

'Genetics does strange things.'

They reached the front door and turned, this time to explore the rooms that opened off the corridors.

The first was small—well, large enough to fit in Lila's Sydney flat with room to spare, but judging from the size of her bedroom at the palace Lila guessed those who lived here would think this room small.

'It's a small *majlis*, a sitting room. We use the same word for our parliament where men sit and discuss things for the good of the country, but here it's where women can gather to chat. Visitors are brought in here, but off this room is the family *majlis* where the women living in the women's house—and the small children who also live here—meet for meals as well as coffee and gossip.'

'But I haven't seen anyone else around,' Lila pointed out. 'Where are the women and children?'

'You are in guest quarters, which are separate, and these days so many of the younger women, when they marry, move into their own homes, like you do in the West. First Mother insisted she have her own home after Father married my mother, so she runs her own women's house, with her friends and family living there. My mother still lives here but she is at the hospital most of the time, and resting when she's home. I live here, with some younger sisters and our...'

She paused, frowning slightly, then finished, 'There are always older relations, and friends who have been here so long they seem like relations, but as well as that there are children. Children are important in our country, so children who meet misfortune, whose parents die or cannot look after them, are taken in by other families and treated as family.'

Lila smiled.

'That's exactly what happened to me so I guess I was unknowingly following tradition.'

They had entered the larger room, lavishly decorated with gilded arches and intricate carpets on the floor and walls. Comfortable-looking settees lined the walls, while thick, velvet pillows from every colour of the rainbow were scattered on the floor.

Lila walked to a window to look out and saw children playing in the courtyard. She was smiling at their antics when she heard Barirah speaking to someone who'd come in.

'Tariq would like to introduce you to his mother,' Barirah told her. 'He is waiting outside.'

'Can he not come in?'

Barirah laughed.

'Into the women's house? It would be more than his life was worth! Come, I'll show you back to the entrance.'

He was a sheikh again, in the snowy gown and headscarf with two thick black cords holding it in place.

Restraining the impulse to drop a curtsey, Lila greeted him with a smile.

'Is this a big deal? Like an official summons?' she asked him, and he frowned at her. 'Well, it feels a bit like meeting our Queen,' she said. 'I'm not even sure I'm dressed appropriately.'

'I'd say it's more she wants to check you out,' Barirah teased. 'She's heard Tariq's squiring around a new woman and a foreigner at that, and wants to take a look at her.'

Tariq shifted his frown to his half-sister.

'Take no notice of her,' he said to Lila. 'She was a troublemaker from the moment she was born.'

Barirah laughed again.

'I'll leave you to it,' she said. 'Good luck, Lila.'

Good luck?

Why on earth would I need good luck?

The woman could hardly suspect me of having designs on her son when we met for the first time yesterday.

Tariq was grumbling under his breath, probably about Barirah's jibes, so Lila hurried along beside him, skipping now and then to keep up. Except one skip went wrong, and his arm shot out to save her from falling.

'Why can't you just walk like a normal woman?" he demanded, glaring down at her.

'Because you stride along as if all the hounds of hell are on your heels, and I have to run to keep up. Or should I be walking two paces behind you in some form of deference?'

He glared at her for a moment but did modify his pace so they crossed the courtyard together, entering an area devoted to roses, the perfumes mingling in the air so strongly Lila had to pause to breathe them in.

'How beautiful,' she murmured, and Tariq's demeanour softened.

'They are my mother's passion,' he said quietly. 'Come, she will be in the arbour outside her room. She likes to be close to them at all times.'

As they approached the rose-covered bower, Lila saw the woman, dressed in a deep pink tunic with a scarf on the same colour wrapped around her head.

'She's beautiful,' Lila murmured, more to herself than to Tariq, although he heard the words.

'She is,' he agreed.

But as Lila drew closer she saw—or maybe felt—a coldness in the beauty, an impression magnified when the woman gave her a look of haughty disdain.

'My son tells me you are Nalini's daughter,' she said, her voice carefully moderated to conceal any emotion.

'It seems I might be,' Lila replied. 'I was young when my mother died so I remember little about her except as a mother, but the name Nalini rang a very distant bell.'

'And are you here hoping to claim some birth-right?'

Lila felt her lips tighten, but the woman was elderly, and she, Lila, was a guest.

'I am here to work in the hospital and in the mobile clinic that will be looking after children who live far from the city's facilities,' she replied, well aware she could do cool disdain better than most people. 'I am leaving tomorrow to visit the nomad camp in the mountains.'

'With my son?'

The steely question shook Lila for a moment, but she came good and looked directly at the woman.

'And a nurse, an administrator, a driver and a guide. I think your son will be suitably chaperoned.'

To her surprise the woman smiled.

'So you've got some spirit, have you?' she asked. 'Maybe you *are* Nalini's daughter.'

Tariq, who'd been about to step in when his mother had asked about his and Lila's trip to the nomad camp, decided it was better to leave with his mother smiling than risk her reverting to her regal hauteur.

'Well, now you've met Lila, maybe you could visit her sometime in the guest quarters. Barirah has put her in Nalini's old room.'

'I can hardly be visiting if she's out at the nomads' camp with you, now, can I?' his mother responded with her usual asperity.

Tariq smiled.

'We're not going out there to live, we'll be back in a few days, a week at the most.'

'Then maybe you will do me the honour of dining with me when you return,' his mother said to Lila, so graciously Tariq couldn't help but feel suspicious.

Time to get the visitor away!

They walked back through the gardens—well, strolled as far as Tariq was concerned—but, surprisingly, he, who usually strode from place to place, job to job, found it surprisingly easy to stroll with this young woman by his side.

'So, tomorrow?' she asked, looking up at him

as she asked the question. 'What time do we leave?'

He was about to suggest eight o'clock when he remembered the sheer joy of seeing the sun rise over the dunes.

'How early could you be up?' he asked, and saw a slight frown draw her eyebrows closer.

'That's the kind of question one should never answer without asking why,' she said. 'Like what are you doing Saturday night, and if you say nothing someone invites you to hear a rock band that blasts your eardrums out. So why?'

He had to smile at her caution, although he knew exactly what she meant. Hadn't he been caught out too many times with an incautious answer?

'Because if we leave early, we can fly out to the Grand Sweep—one of the big dunes—and see the sun come up over the desert.'

Her smile would have rivalled the sunrise and once again he felt something moving in his chest.

'At home a sunrise over the ocean is special, but to see one over the desert? Could we really do that? How early would we have to leave? Not that it matters, I can get up anytime you say.'

The delight of her smile was echoed in her voice and what could he do but smile back?

'Not so early—maybe ready to leave by five-thirty? I will let Sousa know, and arrange for us to take a breakfast hamper.'

'Five-thirty. I'll be there. Front door again?'

He nodded, already wondering if he was mad to have even suggested such an outing.

But it was too late to back out now. Besides, she was a visitor, and all he was really doing was showing her one of the special sights of Karuba.

'I'll see you then,' she was saying, slipping away from him to cross the courtyard to her room, but as he headed back to his quarters, then out to the hospital, the little niggle of doubt about the outing grew into a huge concern, which seemed to be centred on the wisdom or otherwise of sitting on a blanket on the sand with this woman who was already causing too much distraction in his life.

His head told him he was worrying unnecessarily, he barely knew the woman, while instinct suggested that leaving it at 'barely' was a very good idea.

So they'd 'do' the sunrise thing and then get on with their work—strictly as colleagues.

CHAPTER FIVE

LIGHT WAS BEGINNING to seep into the world, stars fading in the sky as it turned from inky black to grey.

Lila waited on the loggia, ready to go. By her feet was her small carry-on suitcase with what she hoped would be enough clothes to see out her visit to the nomad camp.

What had Tariq told his mother about their trip—a week, or had it been more?

Well, everything in the bag could be washed out, and she could alternate long trousers and tunics so really it was no problem.

Expecting a car, she was surprised when Tariq appeared on foot out of the gloom of the court-yard, coming up to her and lifting her bag from the ground.

'We go this way,' he said, and she set off after

him, again hurrying to keep up as he was back in stride mode.

'All the vehicles are kept at the back of the gardens, including the helicopters and small planes.'

He threw the information over his shoulder.

'Small planes?' Lila echoed.

''There's a runway outside the walls and external gates wide enough to wheel the planes out to it,' he replied, as if everyone had a fleet of small planes somewhere on their property. 'They're useful for visits to neighbouring countries, and for showing visiting dignitaries around Karuba. And less noise than the chopper!'

Lila shook her head. The more she learned of this place, the more astounded she was to find that people lived this way—in palaces with planes and helicopters and heaven knew what else just out the back behind the garden.

And took it all for granted!

They came out into an open area, beyond which what looked like garages had been built against the walls of the old fort. There were too many for Lila to count before Tariq had led her to a shiny little bug of a helicopter, painted a dark olive green, the now familiar golden script written on its side.

'Let me guess,' Lila said, running her fingers over the flowing patterns. 'The head must rule the heart!'

Tariq laughed and shook his head.

'No, my sister's idea of a joke. It says "Tariq's toy".'

Could she ask which of the swirls and curves said Tariq?

Of course she couldn't, and she should stop sliding her fingers over the flowing script like some—what?—lovesick teenager?

Surely not!

Of course not!

She barely knew the man...

And still didn't really know herself...

Tariq settled their luggage and opened the door for her to clamber in—thank heavens for long, loose trousers!

It was like being in a bubble, the windows seemed to stretch right around her so she could see the ground beneath her feet as well as the sky above, a paler grey that was beginning to show the hint of colour that would herald the sun's arrival.

The little bubble lifted effortlessly into the air, and as they circled the palace she could see the patterns of the courtyard gardens, the arbour outside her room, and the thick walls of the old fort.

Then they were out over the sea, circling again, this time over tiny fishing boats with odd triangular sails, muted red and faded brown.

They returned to land, passing over the city, and suddenly there it was, the desert.

Breath caught in her throat, and her lungs seized. She told herself that anyone seeing such beauty for the first time would be awestruck, but this was different—this was like coming home, for all she'd never been here.

Shadowed still, grey and black, here and there touched with gold, the dunes rolled away beneath them. The little aircraft tilted slightly, turning towards a dune higher than the rest, curved like a huge wave curling in towards a beach.

With seemingly effortless ease, Tariq set the helicopter down.

'Don't open your door for a minute—let the sand settle,' he said, but he slipped out into the swirling cloud, retrieving a wicker basket from the back and carrying it to the top of the dune.

Lila was opening her door when he returned and dragged a rolled carpet from behind her seat.

'Can I carry something?" she asked, although the question was automatic as she looked around the vastness of the desert, trying to take in its enormity—its magnificence.

'No, just follow me,' he said, so she did, still looking around, seeing the way the wind carved shapes in the sand and feeling how it shifted under her sandals.

The urge to take them off and feel the sand between her toes was too great so, keeping a wary eye out for scorpions, she did just that, surprised to find how cold the sand was, thrilled to feel its softness.

Tariq had spread the carpet, which must have been rolled around some cushions for three of them were cast casually on the material. The hamper was open and from it he'd produced a very beautiful silver coffee pot.

'This is picnicking in style,' Lila teased, unable to hide her delight in what was happening—the dunes, the picnic, the elegant coffee pot. And Tariq, in jeans today, and a leather jacket—was he a desert biker?

'The pot is insulated to keep the coffee hot,' he explained as he brought out covered dishes and set them on the carpet.

'Far more upmarket than the flask I carry when I drive home from Sydney for a visit.'

'So, tell me about your home,' he said, but Lila barely heard the question, for the sand around her was turning to liquid gold, while the sky to the east was flushed with pink and orange, and the tiny curve of the red orb of the sun poked above the horizon.

'Oh!' was all she could manage, and although Tariq pressed a cup of coffee into her hands and passed tempting-looking treats her way, she could only stare as the world was reborn with the sunrise, the colour on the dunes around her changing with every moment that passed.

Tariq watched her face, with expressions of wonder and delight chasing across it.

Emotion, too, for now and then a tear would spill and be swiftly wiped away, but mostly it was awe until the sun was fully up and she turned to him with a smile that lit up the dunes even more than the sun had done.

'That is the most magical thing I have ever seen. Can we do it again?'

He had to smile.

'Well, not right away,' he said. 'It's not a film or DVD where we can press rewind but there'll be other mornings, many of them.'

For some reason he nearly added 'I hope' but pulled it back just in time.

Though why?

Lila was eating now, testing and tasting the delicacies he'd had his cook prepare for them, so he was free to study her—or at least to glance her way several times.

He was too much his father's son—too indoctrinated in the rules of the head and heart—to trust the strange things that had been going on in his chest, *So think with your head,* he told himself.

One, to all intents and purposes she was a foreigner, not brought up in their ways and customs, and there were too many instances of troubled marriages and divorces in his own and his parents' generations that stemmed from marriage to a foreigner.

But setting that aside, there was the turmoil a relationship between the two of them would cause within the palace. Second Mother's hatred of Nalini, whose behaviour had reflected so badly on the new wife, was the stuff of legend, so how would she treat Nalini's suspected daughter?

And on top of that there was the theft.

Though Lila was the innocent recipient of the Ta'wiz, the very fact that she had it pointed to Nalini as the thief. And how would the daughter of a thief—a thief who had brought such shock, and disbelief, and sorrow, to his family—be accepted in palace circles?

He nodded. His head was right. It had come up with very sensible, cogent reasons for not getting involved with this woman and the fact that there seemed to be a physical attraction—the feelings of his chest and elsewhere—underlined the fact that his head was right.

He glanced her way again. She had bitten into a honeyed pastry and was wiping the sweet liquid from her chin with her fingers and licking them. He was close enough to take her hand and lick them clean himself and had actually moved before his head threw up a warning—a definite 'red for danger' sign.

He handed her a damp cloth instead, and watched as she wiped her fingers, then her face, inhaling the scent of the cloth.

'Rosewater?' she asked, waving it in front of her face to intensify the faint perfume.

'Yes. My mother uses it for everything, from perfume and soap and hair shampoo, to cooking and making candles.'

'It's beautiful. Too faint to be overpowering but there to be enjoyed.'

'I hope you find all of Karuba the same,' Tariq said. 'Here to be enjoyed!'

She turned to him with a smile that rivalled the sun with its radiance.

'I know I'll find it the same,' she said. 'This may sound silly, given I've never been here, or really known much about it, but I feel as if I've come home.'

His head told him that didn't mean a thing, but this time it was definitely his heart that reacted for he felt it skip a beat...

'Time to go,' he said, putting a stop to the non-sense going on inside him. 'We've a full day's work ahead of us.'

Lila looked around as they lifted into the sky once more. Sand, sand and more sand, although up ahead she could see the mountains, great, smooth mounds and slices of rock that seemed to have been thrown together or built by some ancient tribe of giants.

'The wind and sand wear the rocks smooth,' Tariq told her, though he couldn't possibly be reading her thoughts. 'But see the green at the base? That's where we're heading. It's a very fertile valley with streams fed by underground springs in winter and snowmelt in the summer.'

Low brown tents, shaped much like some of the rocks on the mountain, appeared beneath them.

'Oh, look, there's our clinic!' Lila cried, pointing downwards, but they were already past, flying over it and landing in a flat field a short distance away.

'Should I cover my hair?' Lila asked, as the little aircraft settled and the engine noise ceased.

Tariq smiled at her.

'Not here,' he said. 'The nomad women are tough and confident, and subservient to no man. You'll see.'

And Lila did see. Women with strong, attractive faces, some wearing lipstick and a slash of red across their cheeks, came forward to meet the helicopter. They wore bright clothes, too, deep blue trousers and dusty red tops, with intricately braided belts around their waists and similar braided cloth wound through their hair.

They greeted Tariq with politeness but not the

deference Lila had noticed at the airport, and she realised that these women would bow to no man.

'They remind me of Barirah,' Lila said to Tariq as she joined him to greet the women.

'Blood kin—your blood too, most probably,' he said briefly, before greeting the woman who stepped forward as spokeswoman for the group.

He introduced Lila then led the way to where the mobile clinic was already set up, with long lines of women and children sitting patiently on the sand outside it.

'Births aren't always officially registered, so our administrator will start there, making a record of every child, their name, date of birth, any previous illness, vaccinations if any, then we add to the record as we see the children as they grow up.'

It sounded simple enough but as Lila looked along the long line of women and children, she wondered if the number of days Tariq had allowed for this visit would be long enough. To get through those already waiting might take weeks.

'Well, best we get started,' she said. 'I imag-

ine some of the children have already been doc-
umented.'

And so began one of the longest days Lila had
ever put in, even back when she'd been an intern
in the ED.

The nurse did most of the vaccinations because
Lila found herself with Tariq in what she thought
of as the operating theatre, debriding wounds and
dressing them, often having to suture the skin
where the wound was too big to leave open.

'This child should be in the hospital,' she said,
when a little boy with bad burns to his left foot
and leg was brought in.

The wound had been treated with something
greasy, which, when cleaned off, revealed a large,
infected area.

'It must be so painful,' she remarked to Tariq,
who shook his head.

'Unimaginably so, but they are stoic people.
He would not let his family down by letting us
see his pain.'

'So, what do we do?'

Tariq was examining the wound very carefully.

'I'd suggest hospital but they are moving on soon and I doubt his family will agree. So we will cut away all we can of the infection, and I'll do a split-thickness skin graft to cover the gap. If I leave a shunt in and give the mother strict instructions how to care for it, the graft should take. We'll be here to watch it the first few days and I can fly back out to check if necessary.'

Lila looked around the makeshift theatre.

'You'll do a skin graft here? How will you take the skin? And the child will then have two wounds that could get infected.'

He looked up from his study of the foot and smiled at her.

'We can do anything,' he said, and something in the way he spoke had her almost believing it.

But the 'we'?

That was a bit odd, wasn't it?

'I'll take skin, dermis and epidermis, from his thigh, run it through the rollers on the meshing device to make it bigger, then we'll fix it over the wound. I think a light general anaesthetic should do him if we've got everything in place. Absorbent dressings for both sites, maybe staples—no, sutures, I think—then thick pressure padding to hold the graft in place.'

'And the donor site? Absorbent dressings? But won't they need to be changed regularly?'

'Yes. We can do that while we're here, then leave them with the boy's mother with strict instructions and also give the female elder the same information. I think they can manage.'

'Antibiotics?'

'We'll start them IV and leave tablets. So, are we ready to go?'

They'd both been moving around the little cabin as they spoke, gathering equipment they would need—well, Tariq had been gathering equipment while Lila watched to see where everything was kept. So much equipment in such a small space!

But she did find gowns and gloves, and the drawers where dressings were kept.

With a heart monitor attached to his chest and a pulse oximeter to one finger, the little boy was anaesthetised, and they began work, first cleaning both the wound and the donor site on his thigh.

'We work well together,' Tariq said at one stage, and Lila looked up to meet the dark eyes above the mask.

It was just a passing comment, she knew that, but she felt a thrill of pride run through her body.

'Bandage both sites well then put a sleeve over them,' Tariq said, as they finished and he concentrated on the slowly awakening child. 'He might rest for a while this afternoon but he'll be out playing with his friends again tomorrow.'

Lila searched through the dressing drawers for the smallest of the long tubes that could be cut into protective sleeves. She cut two and slipped one over each wound, wondering, as she did so, if she should also wrap them in cling wrap of some kind to prevent them getting wet.

'I hope his mother can keep him out of water,' she said, and Tariq smiled.

'We can only do so much,' he said. 'I will speak to his mother about keeping him inside for at least a few days.'

Lila nodded, busy cleaning up while Tariq carried the little boy outside, passing him to his anxious mother, talking quietly to her in a gentle voice—suggesting, Lila guessed, rather than ordering.

'So what's next?' she said, when he came back in.

'What's next might be dinner,' Tariq told her. 'The nurse has already finished for the day. Come, I'll show you to your tent.'

'Tent?' Lila shook her head. 'Yes, of course it would be a tent, I just hadn't thought about it. Is it a women's tent or do you—or these people—have guest tents?'

'Definitely guest tents, although you'll be sharing with Rani and Sybilla. I do hope that's all right with you.'

'Fine with me,' Lila assured him, having already spent enough time with the two women to know she liked them.

He led her out of the theatre and locked the door, then along a path by one of the little canals she now knew ran right through the oasis, carrying water to date palms, fruit trees and vegetable gardens.

Then, on a grassy knoll up ahead of them, she saw one of the low-slung tents with which she was becoming familiar. A taller post held up the middle of the material to form a doorway, before dipping away to where lower posts held the sides about four feet off the ground.

Having eaten lunch in a similar tent, she knew the central area was the living and dining area of the house, while the outer edges made up the sleeping area.

'Your things will be in the area behind the purple curtain,' Tariq said. 'I'm sorry there's no time for you to rest, but you can at least freshen up before we have dinner in the main tent. Everyone will be anxious to meet you and to talk of how happy they are to have the clinic visit.'

Lila laughed.

'And not one word of it will I understand,' she said. 'I should have thought of learning the language before I came rushing over here.'

She'd already ducked into the tent and was

heading for the purple curtain so she wasn't certain, but she thought she heard him say, 'I'm glad you didn't.'

The meal was a riotous affair, with men, women and children all seated on the ground around a large carpet covered with a patterned cloth, on which platters and dishes of every imaginable food had been laid.

She was seated at the side, Tariq on one side of her, Rani and Sybilla on the other. Rani explained the food as each dish was passed to Lila, while Tariq translated bits and pieces of the conversation.

'It's like Christmas at home when all the family come, with the children and in-laws and usually a few neighbours who have nothing else to do. But these people, do they all travel together? And do they always eat together? Is everything shared?'

Tariq smiled at her questions, not a good thing because Tariq's smiles were becoming increasingly unsettling.

'It is how they have survived for so long in a very unforgiving environment,' he told her. 'Sharing builds a bond that is hard to destroy.'

And looking around the happy faces of those gathered on the carpet, Lila could sense the feeling of belonging they all shared. A feeling of belonging she, too, might share.

The thought made her shiver, but in a good way. Testing to see if she was compatible enough to give Khalil stem cells would also give them a picture of her DNA.

Would it match, in part, those of other members of Second Mother's family?

Prove she *was* Nalini's daughter?

Prove she, too, belonged…

Or prove that she didn't.

That thought was like having a bucket of iced water poured over her. To have come this far, found hints and clues, then lose it all and have to start again.

It was a reminder not to get too close—to Sousa, to Barirah, to the people…

To Tariq?

Definitely to Tariq.

The second day was, if anything, busier than the first, as parents who had been too shy to approach the clinic the previous day gained courage from their friends and family and brought along children with a variety of medical conditions.

'Are more people coming into the camp, so that we're seeing children we haven't seen before?' Lila asked on the third day, as Tariq walked her back to her sleeping tent.

'No, it just takes some people a little longer to accept that there might be something wrong with their child, and then to believe we might be able to help.'

They stopped at the opening into the tent, Tariq peering into the darkness within.

'Are you on your own tonight? Would you like me to come in and light the lamps? Check for scorpions?'

Lila's body tensed. They were close enough for

her to pick up the uniquely male smell of him—close enough for the attraction she'd been trying desperately to deny to shiver within her.

But did he mean come in and light the lamps—and check for scorpions—or was he asking something else?

She didn't have a clue, but rather thought the words might be literal.

Which was for the best, for she was still finding herself...

'Or perhaps you'd like to take a walk to the top of the first crest in the mountains, so you can look down at the camp from above?'

Was it just her own attraction that made her want the invitation to be more than a suggestion of a walk? There was only one way to find out...

'Yes, I'd like that,' she said.

Madness, Tariq told himself, walking along the narrow path with Lila close to his side. He knew it was his libido not his heart that drew him to her, but why make things harder for himself by walking with her in the moonlight?

Seeing the way she moved, her body swaying

beneath her concealing clothes as she picked her way along the rocky track.

And the way her eyes widened in delight when she paused and turned to look out over the dunes, silvered by moonlight, rolling on for ever.

Her lips, rosy against her paler skin, parted as she breathed a little gasp of delight.

She was close, so close.

If he bent his head just so—

His head had actually begun to move—to capture those parted lips—when he heard the growl nearby and cursed his folly for coming up the path, putting Lila in danger.

'Stay very still,' he said quietly, sliding one arm around her waist in case he had to lift her to safety.

'What is it?' she whispered, the breath of the words feathering against his neck.

'It's a leopard, possibly a female. We might have ventured too close to where she's hidden her cubs.'

'A leopard?' She paused before adding very softly, 'It means something to me, the leopard. It clicked in my head when you talked about them before, but I can't find the thread to unravel whatever it is.'

'Don't push it and it will come.'

He turned back towards the camp, easing Lila in front of him, keeping her body close to his with his left arm while his right hand broke off a piece of thorn tree.

He knew it would be practically useless as a weapon if the leopard attacked, but he felt better having something he could swing, thrust or throw, if necessary.

They walked slowly at first, not wanting to upset the unseen beast with any unnecessary movement, then quickened their steps as they drew closer to the camp, Lila slipping out of his protective clasp as the ground levelled out.

People were leaving the big campfire, drifting back to their tents in groups or couples, Rani and Sybilla meeting up with them outside their guest tent.

'I hope you didn't walk up the hill,' Rani said, nodding in the direction they'd come from. 'One of the elders was telling us there've been leopard sightings there recently.'

And even in the moonlight they saw the radiance of her smile as she added, 'Isn't it marvellous that they've been saved from extinction?'

'Marvellous,' Tariq echoed drily, before saying goodnight to the women and heading for his own tent.

But the feel of Lila pressed against his body remained with him, and he wondered if he would have kissed her had not the leopard warned him off.

And where kissing her would lead?

She was possibly family, he reminded himself sternly. You didn't fool around with family.

There were plenty of attractive, intelligent women in the city who enjoyed no-strings-attached affairs, women who had their own agendas in life, usually agendas that didn't include marriage.

Marriage…now, there's a thought, a small voice whispered, and he was almost certain it wasn't his head.

Tomorrow he'd talk to the men, check out any health problems, and discuss their plans for the year ahead. With tourism increasing, and more areas under oil exploration leases, these people's lifestyle was changing.

But it shouldn't vanish for ever, and it was up to the government and his father to protect the lands these people roamed.

'Many of the women are fearful for the future,' Lila announced as she sat down next to him at the dinner mat next evening.

He had to smile.

'How have you managed to talk to them to glean that information?'

'Rani translated and some words I know now, but also a number of the women speak English. Apparently they were sent to the city to school so they could learn it, and French as well, which made me feel very inadequate.'

'But not totally inadequate if you've picked up on their concerns.'

He explained how the men felt the same way

and talked a little about the measures that could be put in place to preserve the nomads' lifestyle.

'I'm glad you can do something,' Lila told him, eyes bright with the compliment. 'It's a little like the leopard, isn't it? A lifestyle that's thousands of years old should be saved from extinction.'

'But adapted to modern ways as well,' he argued. 'There's no reason now for children to die from measles, for instance.'

The dark eyes looked thoughtful.

'You're right, of course, but everything's compromise, isn't it?'

CHAPTER SIX

THEIR DAYS PASSED SWIFTLY, and Lila was amazed at how quickly she was picking up the language. Walking with Tariq through a date grove, in a rare lunch break, she said, 'I'm wondering if I knew the language as a child. If both my parents came from Karuba they would have spoken the language.'

Tariq was quiet, but Lila was no longer put off by this man's silences—in fact, she rather enjoyed the fact that they could walk together without need for words. She found it…well, not comforting exactly but right, although the reaction of her body told her walking with him, talking with him, being anywhere near him all held inherent dangers.

Attraction could grow so easily…

But today she had thoughts she wanted to sort out in her head and maybe talking would help.

'When I was found—after the accident—I didn't speak at all, not for months. I clung to Pop, who'd rescued me, and followed him around like a puppy, but I couldn't, or wouldn't, talk.'

Tariq had stopped and turned to look at her.

'And when you did, did you speak in English?'

She thought back, then nodded, adding, 'But the family all spoke English so that was natural, although I wonder if not speaking at first was to do with being bilingual originally? If I'd picked up bits and pieces of both languages then the shock of the accident—of losing my parents— took both languages away, or simply confused me so I didn't know how to talk.'

'So, you're thinking if both your parents spoke Karuban, then your father must also have been from here.'

Lila knew she was frowning as she looked at him, taking in his words.

'But why not? I always assumed he was. Where else could he have come from? Where would my mother have met someone else? Who else could he have been?'

Tariq sighed.

'It could have been a foreigner, someone from a diplomatic posting, even someone working for an oil company—it could have been anyone. All we know is that your mother left alone.'

Which was even more puzzling as far as Lila was concerned. Tariq had walked on again and she reached out to catch his arm.

'But if it was a foreigner, how could he have got into where ever the Ta'wiz was kept? How could he even have known about it, let alone steal it? We need to talk about this. I need to know. If my mother has been branded a thief, I need to know why. As far as I'm concerned, she could have bought the Ta'wiz from someone second or third hand just because it reminded her of home.'

Another sigh, then Tariq led her to a stone step beside the little canal that fed the date palms and, sitting in the cool green grotto formed by their bending leaves, he began to talk, his voice gentle, as if fearing his words would hurt her.

'It wasn't only the Ta'wiz that disappeared, and although it was the most important piece, it was the least valuable in monetary terms. You must understand my family have been guiding traders through the deserts for thousands of years, and grateful customers, I suppose you'd call them, have given my family many gifts. That is what became our nation's treasure—its defence against bad times. And as well as the Ta'wiz, many other things were stolen.'

This was getting worse and worse but Lila wasn't about to give up.

'What kind of things?' she demanded.

'Jewellery mainly—a diamond and emerald necklace, a wide belt studded with precious stones, things that could easily be sold for money.'

'How much money?'

The words were little more than a whisper, but she had to know, and better to hear it from Tariq than a gossiping palace employee.

Another sigh. He wasn't enjoying the conversation one little bit, that much was obvious.

'At the time, over twenty years ago, the total was valued at about five million.'

Lila heard the gasp come out before she could catch it.

'Five million what?' was the best she could manage, knowing Karuban money was of less value than Australian. Praying he was talking Karuban money...

'US dollars,' came the terse reply, and Lila bowed her head, fought back tears, and tried to imagine a theft of such magnitude.

'But...' she said, as her brain began to work again and memories of the gentle mother she'd known came flooding back '...how could my mother—well, Nalini, who probably *was* my mother—have done that? I presume you don't leave millions of dollars' worth of treasure lying around for anyone to pick up. Surely it is kept somewhere special. And she hadn't lived in the palace all her life. You said she'd come with her sister not long before she disappeared.'

A long silence met her impassioned speech.

Maybe he wasn't going to answer her, but at least he hadn't walked away.

Although he did stand up, and put out his hand to help her to her feet.

The touch was nothing more than courtesy, but its warmth flared through her traitorous body.

But focussing her mind on Nalini's supposed crimes helped her squash the warmth he ignited, letting the coldness of defiance and perhaps a little fear take its place.

'The treasury collection is kept in a special room,' he continued, 'a large, walk-in safe, to be precise.'

'And Nalini, who was relatively new to the palace, knew this and could not only find it but get into it. Surely that would have been impossible. I mean, finding it maybe, but getting into it?'

He shook his head.

'No, it was safely guarded and hidden away, looking just like another door in a wall. It is thought she seduced the Keeper of the Treasury, who was my father's youngest brother, and he either let her in or stole the jewellery for her.'

Lila shook her head, unable to believe that the gentle mother she remembered so hazily could have done such a thing.

'Did this Keeper man say that?' she demanded. 'Did he admit the theft? Did he say she seduced him?'

Tariq shook his head.

'He refused to admit to anything. He never said a word. But the loss was put down to him—he was the Keeper after all, so it had been his responsibility. Had he not been my father's brother, had he not been family, he would have been executed. As it was, he was banished from the Kingdom, never to return.'

'But that's appalling! And surely my mother—Nalini—would have known he'd be punished, so I don't believe she'd have let him take that risk. Execution?'

She shuddered.

'This is wrong, I know it is,' she said vehemently. 'I cannot prove it, but I know it's wrong.'

'You were four when your mother died,' Tariq said gently. 'It is hard to judge a person at that age.'

Lila shook her head.

'I might have accepted her taking the Ta'wiz if she was leaving the country she loved, but putting someone else at risk? Even at four you know the essence of your mother.'

'But not her name?' Tariq replied.

'That's unfair!' Lila yelled at him, the composure she'd been clinging to finally broken.

She spun away, wanting to get as far away as possible from this man as she could, but the paths they'd followed were like the labyrinth at the palace and she was uncertain which way to go.

He should let her go, Tariq decided. Let her lose herself in the meandering groves. Rani could help him change the dressings on the boy's wound and donor sites.

How ridiculous to think she could judge her mother's honesty at four!

If Nailini *was* her mother…

Yet hadn't he, at eight, refused to believe the stories that had spread through the palace about Nalini?

Not that eight-year-olds would have much better judgement of character than four-year-olds. It was a gut instinct thing. He'd liked Nalini and hadn't wanted to believe her guilty, and Lila had loved her mother…

He sighed and headed off after her, wondering why he, who rarely sighed, seemed to have made a habit of it lately.

It was the woman, and the way she'd stirred up the past.

Stirred up more than the past?

No, he wasn't going there.

Not catching up with her in the palm grove, he returned to the clinic, to find her sitting on an old carpet in the sunshine outside the door, a small child, maybe two years old, resting comfortably in her lap.

'I think this little prince is the last of the triple antigen recipients, and he didn't even make a sound as he had his needle,' she said, and although he detected a trace of strain in her voice, she smiled brightly up at him.

Too brightly?

'So, we could leave tomorrow,' she added, 'if the young boy's wounds are okay.'

He almost retorted that it was he who made arrangements, but as this mobile clinic was to be her job, she had every right to be taking command of it.

'I'll speak to the driver,' he said. 'We'll re-dress the boy's wounds now, then you, Rani and Sybilla can pack up. Just make sure everything is secure.'

'Yes, sir,' she said, throwing him a cheeky salute, but the smile on her lips wasn't dancing in her eyes as other smiles had, and he knew she was still thinking about her mother and the magnitude of the theft.

And because he didn't believe that the sins of the fathers—or mothers, in this case—should be visited on their children, he said, 'You have done nothing wrong.'

And received a slight rise of her eyebrows in response.

They worked together on the boy, Tariq aware of her closeness as a tingling in his skin, but saying little, both agreeing the wounds were healing well.

He left her in the clinic with Rani and Sybilla and went to speak to the men, intending to sit with her at dinner and maybe take her to join the others by the nightly fire. But dinner found her ensconced between her other co-workers, and it was they who took her to sit by the fire.

Not that it mattered, he told himself. Tomorrow they'd be out of here and he'd see far less of her at the hospital. Life would slip back into its normal rhythms.

But what *was* normal now?

A commotion woke him, yelling and abuse, swearing and cursing, and he left his tent to find a group of men trying to subdue an enraged camel.

'She just went berserk,' one of the men told him, finally fixing a halter around the beast's head and neck. 'She lashed out at her boy then bit the man who went to help. You should see him first.'

Tariq left the men to settle the angry animal, and joined the group gathered around the injured man.

'But that's our clinic driver,' Tariq said to Karam, who was organising the chaos.

'Not only that, but his right hand is injured. There's no way he'll be able to drive the clinic bus back to the city today.'

'You could fly him back then return for us. Take Rani and Sybilla to keep an eye on him on the way.'

'And the next clinic?' Karam asked. 'The timetable is tight enough as it is. It's an eight-hour drive back to town, then the bus has to be re-stocked, and is due to go out again in the morning. You know how people will be travelling to the next camp to have someone check their children. We cannot let them down.'

'Can you drive a rig like that?' Tariq asked him, although he was sure he already knew the answer.

'I can,' said a voice behind him, and he turned

to see Lila, rather bleary-eyed but obviously drawn out of her tent by the commotion.

'Of course you can't,' he said.

'I bet I can!' she replied, and had the hide to flash him a cheeky smile. 'Licensed and all. You can fly the injured man back to town, while Rani, Sybilla and I will start to drive the medical unit back to the city. Then you could find a new driver and fly out to meet us on the road. He can take over, and we'll all fly back with you. That way we don't waste time with the clinic sitting here waiting for a replacement driver. Isn't that best?'

She made it sound so simple, but it had to be impossible—pint-sized little beauty that she was driving a huge vehicle like this one.

'Show me,' he said.

And this time her smile was sheer delight.

'I'm sorry the man was injured but I've been longing to drive it.'

She led the way to the vehicle and clambered inside, sat behind the wheel and looked around her, touching things, feeling the steering wheel, the buttons for the gears, running her hands around the dashboard as if learning the vehicle from touch.

'Do you have a phone with you? Could I call Australia?'

Totally bemused, he handed over his phone and waited as she dialled what seemed like a very long number.

'Pop?' she said. 'It's Lila. I'm sorry to wake you. Yes, yes, I'm fine, but the rig I told you about, I'm going to drive it, and it's left-hand drive. What do I need to think about? What do I need to know? My boss is with me so I'm going to put you on speaker phone so he can hear as well. I don't think he quite trusts me.'

'Don't worry about that little girl driving your rig,' a man's voice, deep and robust, said. 'She's spent more time in the cabs of big rigs than most truckies I know. And, Lila, just get a feel for all the controls and the important thing to remember is that, as the driver, you're always closest to the middle of the road—passenger closest to the footpath side. Remember that and you can't go wrong.'

There was a slight pause before he added, 'You all right, lass?'

Tariq saw the smile that lit up her face, and read the love she had for this man she called Pop.

'I'm fine, Pop, just fine. Love to Hallie and all the others. I'll call you when we get back to town.'

Tariq watched as Lila went through what he supposed was a routine exploration of the strange vehicle then saw her smile as she started the engine.

'Well, are you going to insist on a test drive or get out and let Rani and Sybilla in?'

Tariq knew it made sense, but to send the three women off on such a venture?

'You're right about saving time,' he admitted, somewhat reluctantly, 'but I won't let three women drive along these roads without a male escort, so I'll come with you, and Rani and Sybilla can go in the helicopter. I'll just arrange it.'

He climbed out of the cab and spoke to Karam, explaining what they intended to do, knowing

Karam could fly the helicopter every bit as well as he could.

With that arranged he grabbed the bag he'd packed the night before and returned to the waiting vehicle, looking to see that Lila had done the same with her belongings. He climbed back into the cab again, only to be met by a dazzling smile from Lila, excitement fizzing in her eyes.

'Put your seat belt on,' she told him, snapping her own into place. 'And let's go.'

Not wanting to distract her, Tariq stayed silent until they reached the main road, wide and straight, with very little traffic on it.

'You've spent more time in *big rigs* than *most truckies*?' he said, repeating the older man's words.

His reward was another flashing smile, although her face sobered as she went on to explain.

'My parents' car, when they had the accident, came round a bend in the road right into the path of a big rig like this. Pop was the driver. He always said they must have been from the US or Europe and had forgotten which side of the road they should be on. Anyway, he stopped as quickly as he could but the little car had swerved across the road in front of him and slammed into a tree.

She told the story as one heard many times, but there was still a tremor of emotion in her voice.

'Pop got out and was running towards the car when it burst into flames. He says someone called out "Lila", and that's when he saw me in the back. He got me out then tried to help my parents but it was too late, the fire exploded all around him.'

'Having pulled you out, he kept you?' Tariq asked.

Another smile, this one softer, reminiscent…

'Police came, ambulances that were too late, and a lot of people fussing around, asking questions that didn't make sense to me. I just clung to Pop, and he held me in his arms, soothing me with his voice, telling me everything would be all right. It turned out he was a registered foster parent so the police agreed I could go home with him. Not that they'd have got me away from him. I was like a limpet.'

'So he took you home and there you stayed?'

'At first it was a temporary placement, but Pop had been burned, rescuing me, and couldn't drive for a while, so I had him all to myself. Even when he went back to work, I became so upset at being left behind that he would take me with him. He'd always had children's safety seats in his truck because all the kids liked a ride occasionally, but for the first six months I was with Pop and Hallie I practically lived in the truck.'

'And later?'

Another smile.

'I learned to drive one, we all did, or most of us. Pop always said it was something we could fall back on if other careers failed.'

Tariq laughed. This extremely efficient paediatrician having a truck licence to fall back on should she need it?

Impossible!

But he was mesmerised by her ability, fascinated by the way her small hands with their slim fingers sat lightly on the wheel, barely moving as the vehicle rolled down the long straight road.

Mesmerised by the woman too! With what could only be described as a satisfied smile on her lips, she guided their clinic back towards the city. He'd seen enough of her at work to know she was an empathetic and careful doctor, but this?

She turned and caught his scrutiny, and her smile broadened.

'I'd normally be driving with the radio going, listening to music or discussions and interviews, but as I wouldn't understand your radio, per-haps you could talk to me—tell me stories about Karuba, stories about its past, and where it might be going in the future.'

And so he did, describing the unseen tracks across the desert his family had followed for gen-erations, leading tradespeople and adventurers, protecting them as they travelled to foreign lands in search of treasures unavailable in Europe.

He told how the spirits of their ancestors still continued to guide the people across the desert, protecting them from mischievous djinns who could cause havoc in a person's life.

'And the other stories,' Lila asked, 'the *Tales of the Arabian Nights*—were they your childhood stories as well?'

Tariq smiled.

'Childhood stories and history, too, if some people are to be believed, but I think of them as fairy tales, more like your Brothers Grimm.'

Two hours into the journey and Lila had relaxed enough to enjoy the feeling of power driving such a heavy vehicle always gave her. She knew she was smiling, and Tariq would probably think she was mad, but right now she was locked away in a little bubble of happiness and all she cared about was the road ahead.

Well, the road ahead and the country it ran through.

Karuba! The name had immediately conjured up magic in her mind, but now she was here...

She tried to find the words but all she could think was that it felt like home.

Yet it might not be, she reminded herself, heart

heavy at the thought because if it wasn't she'd have to move on, to leave this place and its people when her year at the hospital ended.

Leave the man who sat beside her, pointing out a dune here or vegetation there...

The bubble of happiness had burst and now a helicopter appeared from the east, growing in size until it was above them, then drifting lightly down to land in the sand at the side of the road about a hundred yards ahead.

Lila dropped down through the gears. She had plenty of time to stop safely, but she felt regret that her little adventure had come to an end, in spite of the less than cheerful thoughts she'd been having. Karam would have brought a substitute driver and she'd be taken home in the helicopter.

Home?

Well, back to either the hospital or the palace, she assumed.

Karam and his passenger were out of the helicopter when she pulled up beside it, Karam talking excitedly to Tariq before he'd dropped to the ground.

Lila clambered down, smiling at the astonishment on the face of the new driver, but he did nod his head as if in recognition of ability.

'I'm telling you she is,' she heard Karam say, and came around the front of the vehicle to see Tariq frowning at her.

'What have I done now?' she asked, not quite defensive but ready to be.

He shook his head and turned back to Karam, speaking in his own language, although Karam's reply was again in English.

'But she is. You brought in that genetic expert from the US and he says it's a match.'

A match?

And suddenly Lila understood.

'My blood? I'm a match for Khalil? You can use my blood?' She was so excited she had to fight an urge to hop or skip, until she remembered the reading she'd done on stem cell transplants.

'But doesn't the testing take longer than this?' she asked, her excitement fading.

'The full donor testing normally does but

Khalil is fading fast and the expert we are using believes you are close enough to give it a try.'

It took a moment for her to consider the other significance of this discovery.

'I'm a familial match?' she asked, her voice faint with the hope she felt in her heart.

'Apparently,' Tariq replied, and now Lila did do the little hop and skip of excitement.

'But don't you see, Tariq? See what it means?'

He obviously didn't for he was looking at her as if she was mad.

'I'm related,' she reminded him, 'so I *must* be Nalini's daughter!'

The wonder of it—of this confirmation—grew inside her like an inflating balloon, making her feel so light she had to fight the impulse to dance around again, and sing and clap her hands and celebrate the certainty that she'd found her mother. That it was no longer a possibility, or even a probability, but proof positive—she was of their blood—she'd found her family.

Tariq paused, looking at her—studying her—but when he spoke it was obvious that he had no idea how much it meant to her, for his mind was still on stem cells.

'Are you sure you want to do this?' he asked, and she felt a little pang of regret that he wasn't sharing her happiness.

Though why should he, who'd always known his mother, think anything of it?

Lila turned her thoughts firmly to the stem cell conversation—she'd have plenty of time later to nurse her happiness, and wonder at the confirmation, and consider where it might lead.

'Of course I'm sure. The only problem will be the injections. I'm very vague about the whole procedure but don't I need to have injections every day to stimulate my stem cells so they enter my blood? Would I be able to have them while on the next trip? We were hoping to leave for the next encampment tomorrow.'

'You don't have to do the next trip,' Tariq told her. 'I can have someone else go. The area is less isolated so it won't be as intensive. It is far better you stay here while you have the injections so your health can be monitored. We also need to know when the peripheral blood stem cells have reached a sufficient level in your blood for you to donate.'

He spoke crossly, frowning as he did so.

'That's okay,' Lila told him. 'But what's your problem with this? Why are you annoyed?'

'Because you shouldn't be doing it. We shouldn't be asking it of you! You're a visitor to our country, a guest!'

'As an anonymous donor would be,' she reminded him, wanting to add 'and a relation' but knowing this wasn't the moment to be pushing family ties.

'It's not the same,' he grumbled, and, puzzled by his reaction, Lila wondered...

'Is it because my mother was a thief? Are you upset that I'll be tainting your brother's blood?'

'Of course not,' he said. 'Such a thought is ridiculous. I just feel it's asking too much of you.'

'I offered,' Lila reminded him. 'Now, let's get back to town so you can start increasing my stem cells.'

He glowered at her, but the clinic truck was

moving away, picking up speed as it went down the empty road, and Lila turned to watch it, a little sorry she'd lost her bubble of happiness.

CHAPTER SEVEN

TARIQ FLEW THEM straight back to the palace, walking Lila to the women's house, where Sousa was waiting for her.

Sousa without her usual bright smile, her face grim with worry.

"What is it?' Lila asked, as they walked down the passage to her room.

'There is talk,' Sousa told her. 'Much talk about you being here, about your mother, the thief.'

'No one has ever proved my mother was a thief,' Lila snapped.

'I know,' Sousa said miserably, 'but Second Mother is spreading terrible stories about her, even claiming that your mother tried to seduce the King, and many people believe what she is saying.'

Lila was surprised to find she felt more puzzled than angry about this latest snippet of gossip.

'But if I'm going to try to help her son, shouldn't she be keeping her thoughts about my mother to herself rather than blackening her name?'

Sousa gave a little shrug.

'You have to understand that morality is very important to us. Women must be virgins when they wed, and things like affairs with other men are still punishable by law. We can choose who to marry, and can divorce our husbands easily enough if they are not kind to us, but the greatest gift a woman can give to her husband is her virginity, and then she must be faithful to him and him alone.'

Well, at least I fit the virgin role, Lila thought as she followed Sousa to her room. Not that anyone here would be likely to marry her, and not that it would make her a great prize at home. Modern men seemed to like experienced women—at least that's what she'd always assumed.

Barirah met them as they reached the bedroom. She looked flushed and angry, and launched into a tirade against her mother and the stories she was spreading.

'Don't worry about them,' Lila told her, putting her arm around the other woman's—her cousin's—shoulders. 'But I do think I should probably move out of the palace to the apartment at the hospital. Maybe then things will simmer down.'

'It's because of the blood,' Barirah said, leaving Lila totally confused.

'What blood?'

'Your blood,' Barirah explained. 'When Khalil first needed stem cells Second Mother was sure she could donate them. After all she was his mother. But a sibling is always a better match so we were all tried first. When those failed she insisted on being tested, but she was nowhere near close enough. Now she's jealous of you, just as she was jealous of your mother all those years ago.'

'All the more reason for me to move out,' Lila told her. 'We can go this afternoon. It won't take long for me to pack.'

'But—'

Barirah looked troubled.

'What is it? Lila asked her, not wanting to offend the woman who had been kind to her.

'It's the Ta'wiz,' Barirah whispered. 'I know this might sound like some ancient superstition or witchcraft to you, but Tariq believes—we *all* believe—that things have not gone well since the Ta'wiz left the palace. It is why he wants you here. He understands it was a last gift from your mother and you do not want to be parted from it, so you must stay here too.'

'That's ridiculous,' Lila muttered, fingering the little locket. 'He's a modern man, a doctor, he'd have a scientific mind. Why on earth does it matter where the Ta'wiz is? I begin injections tomorrow to improve my stem cell count in my blood so living at the hospital would be more convenient. Perhaps I should speak to him.'

Barirah shook her head.

'He is seeing our father at the moment, but I can leave a message that you wish to talk to him.'

Barirah departed, leaving Lila with a decision—to pack her things or not. Actually, it wasn't much of a dilemma as she knew Sousa could probably have everything packed within minutes. So she lay down on the bed that had the cover like her mother's shawl and wrapped it around herself, feeling the embroidery thread slightly rough against her skin, feeling her mother so close she could have wept.

But it appeared battle lines had been drawn by Second Mother and she, Lila, could not afford the weakness of tears.

She must have slept, for the room was dark when she awoke, Sousa little more than a shadow by her door, fingers busy under the glow of a small lamp.

'You needn't have stayed,' Lila told her. 'I know how to reach you now if I want anything.'

Sousa stood and hurried to the bed, turning on lamps as she approached.

'I have a message but I heard about you driving the medical truck and didn't want to wake you.'

'I hope it's a message to say I can move to the hospital,' Lila said, trying to shake the sleep from her mind.

'Oh, no,' Sousa said. 'It is from the Prince, from Tariq. He wishes you to join him for dinner.'

'Where?' Lila asked, knowing it was unlikely he would be asking her to his apartment in the palace.

'At his mother's house—well, in the rose arbour there. She will not be present but you will be chaperoned by servants and she will be close.'

Lila laughed.

'I'm not really expecting him to seduce me, you know,' she said, then remembered the stories circulating about her mother. 'Or me him,' she added, rather sadly.

Surely the stories couldn't be true, because whatever Tariq said about sins of the fathers, she knew the stories cast a shadow on her.

She showered and dressed, tonight putting on a pretty pale pink outfit Izzy had given her, insisting she needed something special for going out. Lila's attention had been so focussed on getting to Karuba, her shopping had been automatic— tunics and loose trousers as suggested by the hospital 'Information for foreign workers' FAQs.

Sousa led her through the garden, to where Tariq waited, a sheikh again, and looking so regal, so magnificent Lila had to distract herself by wondering what he wore beneath the robes.

Surely not anything as mundane as a pair of boxers or jockey shorts.

He showed her to a comfortable settee and sat beside her—far too close given the effect his body always had on hers, and the fact that to-night he was even more magnificent than usual.

'You have had time to rest?' he asked, and she nodded.

'I slept for a couple of hours. I must have been more tired than I thought.'

There, she told herself, *you can manage this. Just perfectly normal, polite conversation.*

'I am glad,' he said, 'for there is something I wish to discuss with you. But we will eat first.'

Lila's stomach cramped immediately. What could he want to talk about that was serious enough she'd need food inside her to consider it?

But as servants were already appearing with an array of dishes, she didn't ask, although she only picked at the cheese-filled dates, and took only a small helping of the couscous and chicken with apricots.

With the servants present, the conversation was formal, Tariq thanking her for driving the truck, saying how pleased he was the trial clinic run had gone so well, discussing the injections she was to have over the next four or five days. Lila responded when necessary but became more and more uptight as she tried to imagine what was coming.

She was beautiful, Tariq thought as he carried on about nothing in particular, wanting—*needing*—to keep some conversation going, if only to distract himself from her beauty. The pale pink of her tunic made her face glow, while the dark plait down her back shone from a recent shower.

He imagined it spread across his pillow, felt himself respond to the thought, and tried to get back on track by asking if she'd phoned her father to tell him all was well.

'I'll do it later, when it's a better time at home,'

she said, but the questions in her eyes had nothing to do with her reply.

Of course she'd be wondering why he'd invited her, but now she was here—here and so stunning—he didn't know how to find the words he needed.

Use your head, he reminded himself, but his head wasn't working too well at the moment, distracted, not by the heart but by his libido.

His guest had finished the meagre amount of food she's served herself and was now looking expectantly at him.

'Did Barirah tell you I wish to move to the hospital apartment, is that what this is about?' she asked, with a no-nonsense, let's-cut-to-the-chase look in her eyes.

He shook his head.

'Well, I certainly don't want to stay here with the stories about my mother growing more insulting every day!'

Tell her, his head said, but his heart was pounding—with apprehension, nothing else.

Well, probably nothing else!

'A problem has come up but I think we can handle it quite easily,' he finally said, then realised he could go no further. By stepping down from his position as heir to the throne, he'd thought he'd escape the tradition of arranged marriage and so avoid the possibility of hurting a woman as his mother had been hurt.

Anger at his father for putting him in this position rose inside him, especially as Lila was looking at him with trust and expectation in her lovely eyes.

How could he tell her of his father's directive?

Explain the duty the felt he owed his father, especially after he'd let him down once before? Hurt her with the alternative he was offering?

She sat watching him, dark eyes scanning his face as if to read his mind.

Dark eyes that saw too much, he rather thought. 'So?'

It might only have been a small word, but it was a demand. *Cut to the chase!*

'Second Mother has been causing more trouble

than you know, done more damage than spreading gossip...'

His words dried up as he thought of the dilemma he would be forcing on this woman who, for all he knew, might have a man waiting for her back in Australia, might have dreams of a *real* marriage, of love and the happy-ever-after endings of his mother's books...

'What kind of damage?'

Direct and to the point, his Lila—only she wasn't his, and even married to him she might never be...

'She has persuaded my father that you are trouble. That you will infect the family, particularly the younger girls, with your Western ways, and cause even more trouble than your mother did. I don't know if my father believes this, but Nalini's departure caused him much pain as he'd arranged a very advantageous match for her, and he felt dishonoured when he had to admit it couldn't go ahead.'

'And?' Lila prompted, obviously aware that there was more to come.

'His ultimatum is marriage or exile. You must understand that, to his way of thinking, once a woman is married she virtually vanishes from sight, so married you'd soon be forgotten.'

There, it was out, and from the look on her face she was even more shocked than he had been when his father had imparted this news to him this afternoon.

'Just vanishes? You can't be serious! And just who does he think I can marry? Should I advertise, or just grab a man off the street, perhaps pay him to marry me?'

Her disbelieving reaction was so heated Tariq had to smile, although it was a weak effort and soon faded.

'Me,' he said baldly. 'You could marry me.'

'Marry you?'

She sounded so incredulous Tariq felt a stab of what could have been pain, but he couldn't think about that now. He had to convince her that it was the answer, because the thought of her leaving—

'Would it be so bad? I know you would not be

used to the idea of arranged marriages but if you want to stay...'

He faltered again, mainly because Lila had leapt to her feet, a pale wraith in the scented shadows of the arbour.

'You'd marry me so I'd vanish from the scene and no longer be an embarrassment? How kind of you, offering me a chance to be a nobody!'

Head, head, head! Tariq told himself, but his head didn't seem to be working tonight.

'You wouldn't be a nobody—you'd be my wife,' he pointed out.

'And I'm supposed to leap about in excitement at that thought? Or am I supposed to feel honoured? To be married to such an important man as Sheikh al Askeba!'

Lila thought she was doing quite well, given the total shock Tariq's words had generated. But yelling at him wasn't enough, not when she felt like grinding her teeth or punching something.

Someone?

But neither option would solve the problem.

Marry Tariq, who'd been forced to offer marriage? Not love, just marriage…

Her heart scrunched in her chest, but that was stupid—this was a land where the head ruled the heart and his head had offered marriage.

But what alternative did she have?

Leave this place that she'd just discovered for certain was her heritage? Leave the family she'd only just found? The family she'd sought for so many years?

But marriage? To Tariq?

A quiver ran through her body at the thought—a quiver she set aside to consider later.

But the alternative was exile!

Khalil was her cousin! There was a possibility, however small, that she could help him.

Could she just walk away?

'It would need to be announced,' Tariq said quietly, his face utterly devoid of expression—a graven mask, his words telling her he assumed she'd accept. 'Though, given Khalil's condition, it wouldn't be a grand wedding, just a quiet ceremony.'

'There won't be any kind of wedding,' Lila told him. 'I don't want to marry you, and you don't want to marry me, and no one can make us.'

Or could they?

She paused, thinking of the story of the Keeper of the Treasure who could have been executed.

Karuba was a different country, with different customs.

'Can they?' she asked, and hated the weakness she heard in her voice.

'They can make you leave. If you want to stay, it is the only answer,' Tariq said, calmly ignoring her question—and her protest. 'You must have already realised that Second Mother is a vindictive woman. She lost face when her sister went missing and was declared a thief, and has never forgiven her. Now you are here, and she is spreading the stories about your mother through the palace. When she heard your stem cells will save her son, her jealousy grew even greater. That is the reason you cannot stay without the protection of a husband.'

This is ridiculous, Lila thought, and that little

skip of excitement that had spread through her body at Tariq's mention of marriage was even more ridiculous. She took a deep breath, telling herself to calm down, then plunged into battle once more.

'But she has already blackened my mother's name, what more can she do to hurt me? Send an assassin?'

She'd expected Tariq to smile, but his face remained sombre.

'I do not think she would dare go that far, but anything is possible. It would look like an accident, of course.'

'Well, thanks very much,' Lila said. 'So I'll be pushed under a bus rather than stabbed through the heart. Anyway, if I move to the hospital apartment, I'll be out of her way and I won't hear whatever gossip she spreads.'

'Except she is at the hospital almost as often as she is in the palace, and you must know that hospital staff love a good gossip.' He paused, studying her intently, before adding, 'Is the idea of marriage to me so repugnant you'd prefer to leave the country?'

The idea of marriage to Tariq repugnant?

Unfortunately she couldn't tell him it was, because the little quiver, the little skip of excitement was still there, bouncing around, causing havoc in her body.

Enough! she told herself. *Think this through. Khalil needs your stem cells. You want to get to know your family. You want to find out who your father was, and if possible clear your mother's name. So packing up and going home isn't an option.*

She glared at the man who was causing all her problems.

'I need to stay,' she muttered, 'and if that's the only way I can be safe then, yes, I'll marry you.' Flinging away childhood dreams of wedding flowers and white ribbons on the church pews and herself in a trailing white dress, she searched her prospective bridegroom's face for any hint of a reaction, but instead was met with graven stone!

'But on one condition,' she added. 'If Khalil dies, then you grant me a divorce.'

He looked puzzled, frowning at her.

'What does Khalil's health have to do with it?' he finally asked.

'Do you really need to ask that? You aren't stupid and must know that if Khalil dies you will have to take on the role of the next king. Would you want a wife so tainted with gossip and innuendo? Would your country want a queen whose name is whispered in the kitchen of every house, in every shop and market stall? What damage would it do to the country you love?'

She didn't add the 'and I'm beginning to love' that popped into her head as she spoke, although it was true.

The blank look on his stern face told her he hadn't considered any of this, though possibly because he couldn't accept that his brother might die, but she couldn't weaken her stance. She might not have been here long but she knew that members of the royal family must be beyond reproach.

'So,' she said, determined to get this over and

done with. 'If you agree to that condition I will marry you.' She paused, thinking of possible consequences—unwanted consequences like falling in love with a man who didn't love her, giving herself to him with all her heart, and then having to leave him.

'I'll marry you but I will not be your wife.'

She turned away, fleeing through the gardens, overwhelmed by the torrent of emotions flowing through her. Excitement, regret, the death of dreams...

For an instant, Tariq watched her go, then sprinted after her, telling himself there was no way she was in danger—and that of course Second Mother wouldn't hire an assassin—but apprehension gripped his stomach until he was close enough to call to her.

Softly so the night was not awakened.

'Lila, wait!'

She halted, a pale ghost in the moonlight, and he came up to her, resting his hands on her shoulders.

'I apologise for upsetting you,' he said, the

words stiff and awkward on his lips because, looking down into the depths of her dark eyes, seeing the creamy skin, and rosy lips, what he really wanted to do was kiss her.

Ask for a kiss?

He was a prince and could ask for what he wanted—

As if!

So he took it, tipping his head forward to capture lips that seemed to tremble beneath his, so he had to add pressure, kissed her harder to stop the trembling.

And to taste her!

To feel the softness of her skin.

To learn her mouth and all its mysteries.

To tell her something with a kiss?

His mind blurred and his head, after some initial muttering, appeared to have gone to sleep, so the kiss was only taste and touch, exploration and learning.

He slid his tongue between the lips that had been taunting him for days, felt the warm softness within, felt her tongue touch his, and her body move closer, now returning the kiss.

It's perfectly natural, quite acceptable, because you're betrothed. His head had obviously woken. Maybe now it would take control.

But when she reached up to clasp her fingers around his face, his chin, his neck, to hold his head closer to hers the better to return his kisses, he was lost.

He clasped her to him, felt her slim body fit itself to his harder planes, knew she'd feel his reaction to the kiss, but *he* knew her nipples had peaked beneath the fine material of her tunic, and were pressed like little stones against his chest.

A marriage in name only?

Al'ama! He would never survive it! To have her close, living in his apartment, and he not able to bed her?

Impossible.

He felt a slight movement as she eased her body from his, looking up into his face, his eyes, so many questions in hers.

Questions he couldn't answer.

He had no idea where the kiss had sprung from.

Certainly not from his head, and although blaming his libido would be convenient, he wasn't entirely sure that was the right answer either.

'I'll walk you back to your rooms,' he said, because what else was there to say?

Thank you for not slapping my face?

Thank you for kissing me back?

He put an arm around her shoulders and drew her close, as he had on the mountain when they'd heard the leopard. It had felt good then, holding her like this, and it felt even better now.

Weird, that was what it was, Lila decided, trying very hard not to snuggle closer to the warm body beside her.

Right out of the blue, the man appeared and in no time at all he was kissing her.

Worse still, she was kissing him back, leaning into him, feeling the strength of his body, the power of his kisses.

She'd had to bite back a whimper of regret as she'd eased away from him, because she was pretty sure kissing Tariq had been the most ex-hilarating experience she'd ever had.

But now, walking back to her rooms, it was as if it had never happened, except for the arm that remained around her shoulders.

Which was very nice, but dangerous, wasn't it, given her decision to not be his wife in the full sense of the word?

Tariq's arm dropped from her shoulders as they reached the loggia.

'Goodnight,' he said, very formal now, the passion she was sure she'd read in the kiss completely gone.

But who was she to be thinking she could read kisses?

Maybe it had just been a run-of-the-mill kiss and she'd been caught up in it because she found him so attractive.

It could even have been a dutiful kiss!

This was a head rules the heart kind of man, so really what else could it have been?

But, damn it all, he *had* kissed her, so why could she not, just quickly, kiss him back?

'Goodnight,' she said, equally formally, but she stood on tiptoe, and kissed him on the lips, felt a quick response, a hand on her shoulder, before she slipped away.

Time enough to ponder kisses when he wasn't around to distract her.

Sousa was waiting in her bedroom, a broad smile on her face.

'So you are to marry the Prince,' she said, clapping her hands in delight. 'And I am to come with you to the Prince's apartments to look after you there. You will need new clothes for meeting people with your husband, important people, and a special outfit for your wedding. Oh, it is so exciting!'

Lila simply stared at the young woman, unable to believe how fast word had spread, even less able to believe the bit of the conversation that had the word 'husband' in it.

'This is crazy,' she muttered, all thoughts of kisses forgotten as she slumped onto the bed, wrapping the spread around her shoulders, silently praying for help and guidance from the mother she'd lost so long ago.

Well, that hadn't gone too badly! The first part of the evening at least, Tariq thought as he watched his prospective bride disappear through her door, then turned to walk back through the gardens. He'd got her to consent to the marriage even if she had made conditions.

The kiss had been strange, coming as it had out of nowhere.

And didn't her kissing him back show some level of attraction between them?

'But I will not be your wife!'

He'd known precisely what she'd meant by that. It would be a marriage in name only.

His head knew that was sensible, but there were other parts of him—not his heart, of course— that felt quite a lot of regret...

Forget it, his head said. *You have to follow this path.*

He didn't *really* believe Second Mother would hire an assassin, but keeping Lila here and therefore keeping her safe had become—what? An obsession?—for him.

And why was that? his head asked, but however hard he tried, whichever way he looked at the question, his head couldn't find an answer.

He left the arbour, entering his mother's apartments, telling her only that Lila had consented to his proposal, neither mentioning her resistance nor her condition that it would be a marriage in name only.

His mother looked at him with troubled eyes.

'You like this young woman?' she asked, and Tariq shook his head.

'The marriage is to enable her to stay, nothing more,' he replied.

'Nothing more?' his mother echoed.

'Nothing more,' Tariq told her firmly, though memories of the kiss flashed like neon lights in his brain.

He said goodnight and left, through the arbour again, walking across the gardens to his own apartment, treading over the mosaic telling him his head must rule his heart, but suddenly uncertain about the validity of the statement, because it certainly wasn't his head that had given a leap of excitement when Lila had agreed to his proposal...

Or when he'd kissed her...

It would be a marriage in name only, his head reminded him, but the stirring of excitement remained.

Perhaps if he concentrated on practical matters...

So, what was next?

Hospital tomorrow, and as they'd made no arrangements about leaving the palace, he would have to send a message to Sousa. Then the first injection of GCSF for Lila. He must ask his expert how the injections were likely to affect her. Should she need to rest, it should be at the hospital where he'd be at hand—along with the expert, of course...

And, no, of course Second Mother wouldn't hire an assassin, but...

For someone whose world had been turned upside down, Lila slept well, waking to find Sousa had already brought in breakfast.

'The Prince will collect you at the front door in an hour,' she said. 'He will take you to the hospital and later, if you are well after the injection you must have, he will send for me and we will go to the shops.'

'But I should be working,' Lila protested, and Sousa laughed.

'You are to be married soon and must learn to obey your husband. And even though he's not your husband yet, I would not like to have to tell him you are arguing with his plans.'

Totally exasperated, Lila pushed the breakfast tray aside.

'This is unbelievable!' she muttered, more to herself than Sousa, for none of it was her fault. 'It's like being back in Victorian times, where wives were forced to obey their husbands.'

She was about to add, 'Anyway, it's a marriage in name only,' but realised such words would echo through the palace within seconds and she didn't want to humiliate Tariq with such gossip.

CHAPTER EIGHT

HE WAS WAITING at the front door, not in the car but on the top step near the sandals. Nerves fluttered wildly in Lila's stomach as she took in the man she was to marry.

Think of it as a job, with him as your boss, she told herself. *It's no different from working for him.*

You can do this!

'Good morning,' she said brightly, then rushed into conversation before he could reply. 'I had meant to look up the stem cell stimulating process last night, but went straight to bed instead. I know the injection has a string of initials, but not having worked on an oncology ward in the last few years, I cannot for the life of me remember them.'

Had his eyes narrowed?

Had he not been prepared for professional conversation?

Surely he hadn't expected a kiss by way of greeting?

She stole a glance at his face as they walked to the car.

No, he definitely wasn't expecting a kiss...

Forget the kiss...

'Granulocyte-colony stimulating factor—G-CSF,' he said, opening the car door for her and waiting politely while she climbed in. 'It's a hormone occurring naturally in the body that stimulates the stem cells to enter the blood.'

'And when there's a sufficient level we're good to go?' Lila asked, as he joined her in the vehicle, settling himself behind the wheel, not sparing her a glance.

Perhaps he's feeling as awkward as I am, she thought, but another stolen glance at his face suggested he was as devoid of feelings as the large wooden gate through which they were passing.

She doubted he did awkward!

But she wasn't going to ride in silence.

'And the procedure to harvest them… There's a machine, isn't there, that takes my blood, sieves out the stem cells, then gives it back to me? I spent time with oncology patients during training, but, as I said, I haven't worked with them since. I do remember seeing someone sitting in a collection centre with tubes in both arms and knew he was a donor.'

'Peripheral blood stem cell collection, or PBSC, it's called,' he said, his attention so focussed on the very quiet road ahead it was as if he'd never driven it before. 'It usually takes four to five hours.'

'And the patient?' No way was Lila going to be put off by his lack of conversation. 'There's a risk of graft versus host disease, isn't there? Khalil will need a lot of preparatory treatment before he gets the transplanted cells, won't he?'

'A lot,' was the answer, and Lila gave up.

They were driving down the avenue of eucalypts, and a sudden rush of homesickness washed over her.

She had family who loved her at home—did she need another one?

She could have the injections, donate her stem cells, and then go home—out of Second Mother's way, satisfying the King, and, most importantly out of this man's way—not way so much as presence.

Powerful presence!

Even sitting in a large vehicle with him had the fine hairs on her arms standing up, and little shivers of something—she wasn't sure what—trickling down her back. How much worse would these physical symptoms be when she was married to the man?

A man who didn't love her...

Tariq drove, aware as he'd never been before of the woman by his side. Sitting there, chatting, as if nothing at all had happened between them.

Well, had anything?

Not really—a kiss, nothing more.

So why was his body throbbing with need, his nerves as taut as the ropes on a tent in a storm?

The kiss had obviously affected him far more than it had affected her so that she could carry on a normal conversation—a little stilted, but still—while he could barely think.

Barely think of anything beyond how soft her lips had been, how slight her form when she'd leaned into him, how sweet her mouth...

He was, of course, magnifying the whole thing out of proportion, his head told him, but it was his body doing the remembering, and while the head might rule the heart, it wasn't having a lot of success ruling his body.

There was a lane up ahead that led to a date grove. If he pulled in—kissed her just once more—surely that would release him from the spell, make him realise she was just another woman and all women were good to kiss.

Well, all young, attractive women...

He didn't pull into the lane.

Instead he tried to think about the day ahead, settling Lila for her first injection, making sure she had someone with her, a cup of tea or cool drink, whatever she wanted...

After which he'd send her home or to the big mall where Sousa, and Barirah if he could get hold of her, would organise a wedding dress. He supposed the big mall was where women bought wedding dresses...

His body tightened at the penultimate word and he reminded it sternly the marriage would be in name only.

He glanced her way, and thought he read sadness in her face, the rosy lips downturned, a hint of moisture on her cheek.

Had he been too abrupt? Too unyielding in his response to her attempts at conversation?

Maybe if he tried conversation, the tension in his body would ease.

'I know we kept records of the clinic visit to the mountains but I wondered, when you've time, if you could do a report on it? Aspects you found worked well, any problems that could be fixed, improvements that could be made. Just a general report.'

She glanced towards him and he wondered if she realised he was just making conversation.

'It appears I'll have nothing *but* time,' she said, 'if someone else is taking the next clinic run. I'll be happy to do a report, but I'll need more than that to keep me busy. One injection a day hardly constitutes a full day's work.'

'It's only for four days—or five if we count the day they take your blood. And you'll have the wedding to prepare for. I thought on the fourth day of the injections, that's if they're not affecting you, I should speak to your father—to the man you call Pop. Would you like me to send a plane to bring him and his wife over for the ceremony?'

Lila thought of the crazy, happy day when all the family members they could muster had celebrated Izzy's wedding, and shook her head.

'I wouldn't like them to be part of a pretence,' she said quietly.

He didn't answer, not for what felt like several very long minutes, then, with a sideways glance at her, said, 'It doesn't have to be pretence.'

His voice had seemed deeper than usual, and slightly husky, and it caused such a riot of emotions in Lila's body she was dumbfounded.

Of course it does, was what she should have said, but the words definitely didn't come out.

Instead she looked out the window and thought of the kiss, and where such kisses might lead if it *wasn't* pretence!

They were passing a residential area, substantial rendered brick buildings suggesting wealth, then the occasional flag flying from a pole at the front told her it was probably an embassy enclave.

She looked for the so-familiar Aussie flag, but failed to find it. Perhaps Karuba was too small for an Australian embassy, but surely there'd be a consul? Could she ask him to her wedding, so she had someone from home by her side? She had no idea what a wedding here entailed, even whether they had guests, but surely there'd be witnesses.

'I will take you to the pathology department and introduce you to Professor Eckert, who is both caring for Khalil and pursuing further study into the treatment of childhood leukaemia, especially the use of stem cell transplants. Much of his work has been done with donors who are not a perfect match during the tissue typing tests but who can still successfully donate, given the right preparation for both donor and recipient.'

Lila thought of the implications of this work and felt a little bite of excitement—intellectual excitement this time.

She couldn't help but smile.

'How wonderful it would be if he could make stem cell transplants successful with even, say, a fifty percent match. How much hope that would give people worldwide.'

'He's getting close,' Tariq told her, and he, too, smiled.

Pity, because his smile really did affect bits of her she didn't want affected, so she was distracted when he spoke again.

'After the pathologist is finished with you, you can go shopping,' he said, and, for pity's sake, he smiled again.

'You say that as if it's a great treat,' she muttered, more upset by two smiles in a minute than the actual words. 'As it happens, I loathe shopping. It always seems to me to be a total waste of time. In fact, since I've discovered online shopping, I rarely venture into actual stores.'

This time he laughed!

Not much of a laugh, more a huff of merriment, but if smiles were affecting her, the huff and the twinkle in his eyes that accompanied it were far worse, so by the time they drew up at the hospital entrance she was in a total dither.

Made worse when the words he'd spoken earlier—It doesn't have to be a pretence—had now lodged in her head and become a kind of chant…

Of course it had to be pretence.

Apart from everything else, she still didn't know entirely who she was.

Okay, she had a mother—but her father?

'Are you coming?'

He'd left the vehicle to be ferried away by a doorman, and was standing beside her, peering at her as if he'd like to have read her thoughts.

Good thing he couldn't!

Now he took her arm—because she hadn't answered?—and led her into the hospital.

'Barirah will meet you here when you are

done,' he said, depositing her in an inner office behind the large waiting room. 'I'll wait and introduce you to Professor Eckert, then must do some work.'

It was on the tip of her tongue to tell him not to let her keep him, because his hand was still on her elbow and his body was very close to hers, and what with the kiss and all the other stuff going on, this was not good.

It *does* have to be pretence, she was reminding herself when Professor Eckert arrived.

After two hours of intense scientific conversation with the professor, Barirah's arrival was such a relief Lila didn't complain about the shopping. A car was outside the staff entrance, Sousa waiting in it. Barirah spoke to the driver, and they were swept away, out of the quiet hospital environs and into the chaos of the city, a place Lila hadn't yet seen.

'Busy,' she said, and both women laughed.

'Today's a quiet day,' Sousa told her. 'There are days when cruise ships dock in the harbour and every trader from miles around sets up stalls on the footpaths.'

'And spill over into the street,' Barirah added. 'Normally we don't shop in shops.'

She chuckled.

'That sounded stupid, didn't it? What I mean is the places we, the family, use know all our sizes and also our preferences and style of clothes so they bring selections to us. From today, they will do this for you as well, but they need to see and talk to you, to measure you, and for you to try on different outfits so they will know what to send to the palace.'

'I'm not a good shopper,' Lila told her, not going to far as to say she hated it because Sousa was so excited, and even Barirah seemed happy to have been given this task. 'But I'll go with the flow.'

The car pulled up under the portico of what looked like a very flash hotel.

'They have an arcade underneath with some of the best women's clothing in Karuba,' Barirah explained, while Sousa's eyes grew round with amazement.

'I thought we'd just be going to the mall, but this place?' she said.

Lila smiled. At least someone was happy about today's outing.

But once inside, an unfamiliar excitement stirred in her as well. The clothes were so beautiful, the fabrics so fine, the embroidery so exquisite, Lila found her breath catching in her throat as she looked at the outfits.

'Wedding first,' Barirah announced. She spoke quickly to the manager who had been summoned to give them personal service. The manager passed on the message and within minutes two younger women had appeared, each carrying an armful of beautiful clothing.

It was all hung in a room larger than Lila's bedroom in her old Sydney flat, and she was ushered in, refusing help with dressing, too embarrassed by her clean but practical underwear, and the thought of anyone seeing her dressed in some of these fantastical creations.

But one dress drew her to it, a fine cream silk, its long slim lines appealing to her, the simplicity of its design leaving the embroidery to make it special. The moonflower vine design crawled and twirled thickly around the hem, some tendrils reaching as high as her waist. The embroidered flowers were echoed in the sleeves, close fitting to the elbow, then swelling out to fall in a graceful fold beneath her forearms and hands.

She tried it on and smiled at her reflection, ignoring the knocks on the door and the pleas of Barirah and Sousa to let them see.

Maybe when she went home she could take the dress, show her family…

But the thought of going home—even with the dress—no longer brought excitement and she shook her head when she realised just why that was. There was something about the man she was about to marry that was getting under her skin, and not just in purely physical terms, although that part was becoming more and more distracting.

She dressed in her own clothes again and emerged from the room, the dress in her hands.

'This one is fine,' she said, definitely understating how excited it had made her feel. 'That was easy. Can we go now?'

There were howls of protest from all three women. It seemed the dress needed sandals and a small handbag to match it, and then she would need formal outfits for palace dinners and casual outfits for lunches with her husband.

She stopped listening to the list of what she needed, her thoughts flying to the pink sand. Tariq had said he would take her to see it.

Would he?

She would need a box like the one her mother had always carried, so she, too, could have pink sand to remind her of this strange and wonderful place.

It seemed like hours later that Barirah called a halt to the shopping, perhaps realising just how exhausted Lila was feeling.

'Come, we shall have lunch at the hotel and by the time we get home, everything will have been delivered to your rooms.'

She bustled away to speak to the manager, then

led Lila out into the arcade and along it towards the lobby of the big hotel.

'Is Sousa not coming?' Lila asked when she realised the young woman was not with them.

'No, she will supervise the packing and delivery of the garments and return to the palace to unpack them.'

She led Lila into a small dining room, and to a table in an alcove looking out over beautiful gardens. Amazed again at the beauty and intricacy of garden designs in Karuba, Lila stood at the window trying to take it all in.

So it wasn't until she heard Tariq's voice that she realised he had joined them.

Barirah's whispering to the manager now made sense, but if sitting in a vehicle with him so close this morning had been torture, to sit with him at a small table, even chaperoned by Barirah, would surely be worse.

She turned from the window and he greeted her with a smile.

Damn him and his smiles! Did he not know how potent they were?

She smiled back, but knew it was a pathetic effort, so sat down at the table and searched her mind for easy, undemanding conversation.

'How was Khalil this morning?'

He shook his head.

'Not well, but that's largely because of the preparation they need to do for the transplant. He needs chemo to kill off his own stem cells and antibiotics to ward off infection, so his body, which was already weak, is even more weakened.'

Tariq knew his words were flat, but couldn't rouse himself. Second Mother's histrionics at the hospital this morning were still vivid in his mind.

But Barirah must have picked up on his despair.

'What happened?' she asked him—demanded, really.

He stifled a sigh. He really wasn't a sighing person. He was a getting on with things person.

'Second Mother?' Barirah asked, and the empathy in her voice made him nod.

'Drama?'

'Of course,' he told his half-sister. 'Apparently

we're now all in a plot to kill Khalil. I am the leader of it, but you, I'm afraid, have also been drawn into it and will feel the force of her ire.'

He reached out across the table and touched Lila's hand.

'I am sorry you have landed into the middle of this family furore,' he said, and felt her fingers move, her hand turning so she could give his a light squeeze before withdrawing it and hiding it out of temptation's way under the table.

'It's understandable she is so upset,' Lila said, 'with her son so ill. But does she have the power to stop the treatment?'

Tariq studied the woman he was to marry in a couple of days' time. She looked weary and he wondered if he should have made her rest after the injection.

She raised her eyebrows and he realised she was waiting for a reply.

'No, our father is the final authority but he has given me full rein in deciding who will treat Khalil, and how, and when. Professor Eckert is the best in his field and he will do everything in his power to save him.'

He smiled at her, at this woman who was unsettling him so much, and added, 'With your help, of course.'

But there was no answering smile and he wondered what she was thinking. How could he know? How could he even guess? They were strangers, growing up with different ways and different cultures, no common thread except the thread of blood that ran through all the Karuban tribes.

'Was your shopping successful?'

This time the response was better, although definitely negative if the face she pulled was anything to go by.

'Ask Barirah,' she said. 'I am really not a shopper, and wouldn't have had a clue what I needed without her help.' She paused, smiling at his half-sister, before adding, 'Although I'm quite sure I won't need a quarter of what she's insisted I buy, and I think you'll probably have to raid the Treasure Room to pay the bills.'

'That's nonsense,' Barirah told him. 'She's the most obstinate woman I've ever met. She refused more clothing than she agreed to. Just you wait until you're married and you'll see.'

Just you wait until you're married—the impact of the words ran south through his body, ignoring his head, which was reminding him of his bride-to-be's conditions.

A waiter hovered, ready to take their order, and conversation ceased as they checked the menu and decided on their meals.

He heard Lila's order for a Caesar salad and protested that she should be eating more to keep her strength up.

Her response was a more genuine smile than the one she'd given him earlier.

'It seems I never stop eating here,' she said. 'Sousa stands over me while I eat an enormous breakfast, Professor Eckert pressed tea and cakes on me, and I have no doubt that there will be afternoon tea and then an enormous dinner before the day is done.'

Tired though she looked, the smile lifted her

face and even sparked her eyes, and his desire for her grew—his head powerless to stop it.

Rational conversation, it reminded him, when it realised it had failed to control his desire.

'It is because we have known bad times,' he said. 'When food is plentiful we eat. It was always the way, back through the generations. We build up stores of energy for when things are bad, when crops fail or the winter lasts longer than we were prepared for.'

She nodded, as if she understood, and he wondered just how much of their ancient ways ran through her blood, and who her father might have been. A foreigner would mess with the blood line, but had he been Karuban, then the history of the people would be in her blood.

'Well, fun though this has been, I have to return to work,' Barirah announced when the meal was finished. 'Tariq, you'll see Lila safely back to the palace.'

Tariq caught the look Lila shot his half-sister.

Traitor, it seemed to say, but she didn't argue, simply walking with him out of the restaurant, waiting by his side until the car appeared, then climbing in when the doorman opened the door for her.

'You are tired?' he asked, as he settled behind the wheel.

'A little,' she admitted. 'Shopping is a rare experience for me, and shopping to that extent is so far beyond anything I have ever known, I'm probably more overwhelmed than anything.'

He glanced her way, wondering what her life had been like. Growing up in a foster family, any number of children to feed and clothe, there was no doubt money would have been tight.

Yet she spoke with love of her family, and with devotion when she mentioned Pop.

'You had a happy childhood?'

Her face lit up, banishing the tiredness.

'The best,' she said, 'although I felt the loss of my parents and wondered so often about them, the house was filled with noise and laughter, and with love. We were all so different, yet the bond between us was unbreakable. The musketeer thing really, all for one and one for all, I suppose because the other kids at school and in the town saw as different—the foster kids at The Nunnery.'

'A nunnery?'

She smiled at his astonishment.

'It was where we lived. An old nunnery, a big old building, as forbidding looking as the outside walls of the palace, but inside it was full or warmth and happiness and I was lucky to have been part of it.'

Lucky? When she'd lost her parents?

For her to feel that way, her foster parents must have been truly special.

They were driving down the avenue of eucalypts, and he realised they always seemed to take her home, for once again there was a trace of moisture on her cheek, surreptitiously wiped away by a forefinger.

Was he wrong to keep her here? To want to keep her here? If Khalil lived, should he still set her free?

A wrenching twist in his belly told him no and, as far as he could tell, his head had no answer...

CHAPTER NINE

COULD A WEDDING day be a day just like any other day? Should it be that way?

Her sister Izzy's wedding day had been bedlam, mainly because so many of the family had managed to be there for it, and fitting everyone back into the old nunnery had been chaotic to say the least.

But today, for all Sousa's excitement, felt like any other day to Lila. She was up early, met Tariq by the front door, was driven to the hospital for her injection, then actually spent a quiet hour working on her report of the clinic run.

She was so absorbed in the paperwork, in trying to think of ways they could do things better, that Barirah's arrival in the little office startled her.

'You're getting married in an hour,' Barirah reminded her. 'I'm to take you home immediately.'

Realising it would be futile to argue, Lila went along with her, although now she was not distracted by the report, the butterflies that had been causing havoc in her stomach for the last few days returned a hundredfold.

'I don't even know where this wedding is happening,' she told Barirah.

'You'll see,' her friend replied. 'It is all arranged.'

'But small, no big fuss?' Lila asked. 'Tariq said small.'

Barirah laughed.

'A small wedding here means maybe a hundred guests rather than a thousand, but Tariq insisted it was a private arrangement between the two of you and should remain that way. So, yes, it will be exceedingly small—an exchange of vows, nothing more.'

Lila nodded, content that she didn't have to face hordes of people she didn't know but who would, for sure, have heard the stories of her mother.

'And where is to be held?'

'You will see,' was all Barirah would tell her.

And see she did!

Once bathed and dressed in the beautiful gown, Barirah led her to the front door, family members and staff peeking through doorways, oohing and aahing as she passed, some even murmuring English words like *beautiful*.

It was the dress, Lila told herself, but she knew it suited her, and hoped Tariq would think her beautiful in it as well.

Though why care?

It was a pretence, a marriage in name only, protection for her from an honourable man.

Sousa was waiting by the car, something in her hands.

'A bridal gift,' she said, and lifted a shawl in the same pale green as the bedspread but embroidered with the moonflowers.

She lifted it to drape it over Lila's hair, left loose and falling down her back, and twisted the length of material beneath Lila's chin, throwing the ends back over her shoulders.

'It was how my mother wore the scarf, and is so

very, very beautiful.' She hugged Sousa, thanking her, fighting back tears. 'You made it?'

'You deserved it,' was all Sousa said. 'Now go and marry your Prince!'

And while those words caused a silly weakness in Lila's knees, and although she really wanted to see how she looked in the scarf, she went, aware the pale green of the filmy material would pick up the green embroidered leaves in her dress, and perfectly complete her bridal appearance.

She slid into the waiting car, Barirah by her side, and they drove out of the palace and along the avenue of eucalypts.

Except something was different. Up ahead, where the trees had been planted off to one side to make a shaded picnic spot, stood a tent—the faded brown structure familiar to her now, a tall pole holding it up at the front to provide a door, the material sloping downwards to the lower poles on each side.

It was such a pleasing shape, Lila had to smile, imagining a family gathering there, maybe having a picnic or even camping out a few nights, as the sea was within walking distance, and the dunes behind the tent would provide children with hours of fun.

But the car was slowing, now turning towards the tent, and closer to it Lila could see a brilliant textured carpet spread before the tent—crimson, and gold, with patterns of green and blue woven through it, one of the loveliest carpets she's seen so far in her stay in Karuba.

'We're stopping here?' she asked.

'We are indeed,' Barirah told her. 'For many years the King has had his nurserymen collecting seeds from the eucalypts and now some of the seedlings have grown tall enough to make a bower around the tent.'

The homesickness she usually felt as she drove down the avenue was forgotten, as was her wedding dress, and Barirah, even Tariq. She slid out of the car and went to see the saplings, straight and sturdy, each in a magnificent pot, circling the carpet like a loyal army.

'I thought you might like a touch of home.'

Tariq's voice came from the doorway of the

tent, and she turned to see him standing there, and she hurried towards him, tears streaming down her face.

'This is so wonderful,' she said, smiling through her tears, while he retrieved a handkerchief from some hidden pocket of his robe and held her face while he mopped up her tears. 'You are so kind, so thoughtful of me, I don't know how to thank you.'

He smiled gently down at her.

'Marrying me is thanks enough,' he said, and for one heart-leaping moment she wondered if that might be true.

But no, she reminded herself as she stepped away from the touch that turned her bones to water and her brain to mush, *he's marrying you to keep you here, to help his brother. He's a head before his heart man, remember!*

Another robed man appeared from inside the tent, then Tariq's mother, who looked Lila up and down and then nodded as if she approved of something—probably the dress!

Barirah was to stand beside Lila as witness, First Mother witness for her son.

The ceremony was short, although the official spoke the words in English and Karuban, and when it was done, a servant brought cushions from inside the tent, setting them on the carpet for the guests, before bringing coffee pots and cups then trays of food.

'You must feed your husband before you eat yourself,' First Mother instructed Lila.

Always? Lila wondered.

'On your wedding day,' Barirah explained, as if she'd guessed at Lila's thoughts.

Lila selected a date stuffed with cheese and with her fingers trembling held it to Tariq's lips.

He bit into it, his lips against her fingers, sending shivers of what could only be desire spiralling through her.

And when he took the rest into his mouth, her fingers were caught there, and gently sucked, and for a moment the physical thrill was so intense Lila feared she might faint or at least do something foolish like throw herself into his arms.

'Now I feed you,' he said, his voice so deep and husky it exacerbated all the excitement in her body.

'A small morsel of meat to keep your strength up,' he said, lifting a tiny meatball from a platter, dipping it in yoghurt, then raising it to her lips.

Her mouth opened automatically, but by now she was trembling so violently Tariq had to steady her with his free hand, placing it against her cheek while he popped the little piece of food into her mouth.

Chew and swallow, she told herself, and tried desperately to do just that. Choking on a meatball on her wedding day would be just too bizarre!

And in front of First Mother!

But by now the other women were also eating, chatting to each other as they helped themselves to food.

Tariq poured a tiny cup of the thick rich coffee and passed it to Lila, leaning towards her as he did so, murmuring, 'You look unbelievably beautiful.'

She met his eyes and read the same admiration

there, but she couldn't let his compliment undo her. This marriage was a pretence...

'You've brushed up pretty well yourself,' she said lightly, and saw the glitter of excitement fade from his eyes as he accepted her words as a reminder that it *was* pretence.

The talk became general, as they ate and sipped at coffee, First Mother enquiring about the process of stem cell collection, about Khalil's health, even asking Lila about her family at home.

And sitting on the crimson carpet, familiar gum trees all around her, Lila found it easy to talk of home, of her sisters and brothers, her foster parents, and the little seaside town of Wetherby that had become her home.

Tariq listened, drinking in as much information about this woman who was disrupting his life as he possibly could; seeking knowledge that might help him work out what made her tick.

And possibly what made her so undeniably attractive to him.

There had been other women, many more beautiful—or so he'd thought until she'd appeared today in a silky gown that flowed across her body, the flowers of the dunes embroidered on it. While the scarf that covered her lustrous hair and framed her beautiful face completed the picture of a bride.

No woman could be more beautiful!

Or more desirable.

His body twisted with a hunger he'd never known before, and he wondered how he would manage with her living in his apartments, so close and so untouchable.

Was he mad to have embarked on this venture, this union?

He was considering an affirmative answer to this question when he realised the alternative had been unthinkable.

No way could he have let this beautiful, vibrant young woman disappear from his life.

A car drew up and he knew it was time for he and Lila to go back to his apartments, First Mother and Barirah following in another car.

'Sousa will have moved all your belongings

to your new room,' he told Lila when they were seated in the vehicle.

Lila smiled at him.

'She'll have needed a very large truck with all the garments she and Barirah insisted I buy. If I live to be a hundred I doubt I'll wear them all.'

'Most women would be delighted with new clothes. Do they not interest you?'

She shook her head.

'It's not that they don't interest me, it's—I suppose it's to do with thrift. We weren't poor, growing up, not dirt poor. But Hallie had to be careful with money to keep us all fed and clothed. Most of my clothes were hand-me-downs,'

'Hand-me-downs?' The phrase puzzled him.

'Things my older sisters had worn. Oh, we had special clothes that were just our own, but as long as we had something to wear for any occasion—a good dress for going out, a special dress for special events—the rest were just...'

'Hand-me-downs,' he finished for her, and was pleased when she chuckled.

They rode in silence for a while, her thoughts,

no doubt, back at home with her family—remembering her childhood—while his were on her.
Her quiet beauty, the simplicity of the life she'd
known—and, sneaking in, too powerful to stop
even as thoughts—the desire he felt for her.

Battling these carnal thoughts, he was startled
when she spoke again.

'Thank you for the trees,' she said, the warmth
in her voice underlining her sincerity. 'That was
a thoughtful and wonderful thing for you to do
for me. They made me feel at home, relaxed, and
able to carry on.'

The little smile hovering around her lips told
him just how much she'd loved the gesture and
he was pleased.

Pleased also by a sudden new thought.

'Those saplings are now strong and tall enough
to be planted in a garden. There is a spot at the
back of my apartments where they could be
placed, to make a small eucalypt forest for you.
Would you like that?'

And if I give you these trees from your home-

land, would you stay? The thought flitted through his head—definitely through his head.

'It would be lovely,' she said, 'and even if I didn't stay, maybe I could visit.'

'I'd rather you stayed,' he said quietly, and she turned to him, a slight frown puckering her brow.

'But you married me to save me from exile. At some point you will want a proper wife.'

He paused, wondering if one more push would be too far...

But had to say it anyway.

'You could be a proper wife.'

Lila sighed, then shook her head. Why was he making this so difficult? Saying things that made her think maybe he felt something for her—perhaps something of the attraction she felt for him...

Could she explain?

Would he understand?

He'd been so good to her, and the trees had shown that he had an understanding of her that she hadn't expected.

'I'd like—' she began, but they were turning

into the palace grounds, through a gate she hadn't seen before.

Tariq touched a finger to her lips.

'Wait, for we can talk in private when we are home,' he said. 'We will sit and have a cool drink and you can tell me what you'd like, and I will do everything in my power to make sure you get it.'

She was pondering his words, which had sounded very like a promise, when Sousa met her at the door and led her into a new suite of rooms, beautifully decorated, and, to Lila's delight, she saw that the bed was draped in the cover from her previous room.

'I knew you liked it,' Sousa told her. 'So I brought it with us.'

Lila smiled her thanks, and sank down on the bed. She had to shower and change, ready to meet with Tariq in his arbour in an hour and a half, to have dinner with him, as his bride!

But she felt that the moment she could have explained her abstinence from sex had passed and she wondered if she'd ever find the courage to tell him—to explain...

Tariq sat in his bedroom, his head in his hands, thinking how beautiful his bride had looked, the longing to touch her and hold her in his arms so strong he wondered if it might tear him apart.

He understood the caveat she had placed on their marriage, and his head even acknowledge there was some truth in it—a royal wife should be above reproach.

But she was! he argued. It was her mother, not her, who had stolen from the treasury, and, if truth be told, that had never been proved.

But for now Lila was his, only a short distance away, perhaps peeling off that glorious creation she'd been wearing—the sight of her had stolen his breath. Was she now in underwear, wondering what to wear to dinner, maybe not in underwear, maybe showering?

His body ached with longing, to be with her, near her, touching her.

Peeling off her clothes…

Enough!

She felt it too, he was almost sure of that.

Almost!

Hadn't her lips trembled when he'd fed her, hadn't her hand quivered in his as they'd taken their vows, hadn't she leaned into his kiss—kissed him back?

Of course she must feel it, only mutual attraction could be this strong, although she probably wasn't picturing him in his underwear!

So what did he do?

Ensure his brother lived?

Hadn't that been his first priority since first Khalil had become ill?

So now he had to try harder.

Tomorrow was the last injection, then, providing all was well, the stem cells would be collected the following day.

A sourness in his belly made him wonder if he'd done the right thing, allowing Lila to be used this way. What if she came to harm? Nothing in medicine was foolproof and although she hadn't, as yet, reacted to the injections, draining her blood was a whole different matter.

Cursing himself for his lack of direction—for his uncharacteristic, less than positive thoughts—

he rose, showered, and dressed comfortably. It wouldn't be formal, this first dinner they shared together.

She appeared from the garden, dressed in a dusky blue tunic with matching pants, but both were trimmed with tiny patterns in silver, and the moonlight made them gleam as she moved. Her hair was down, also gleaming in the moonlight, looking so soft and lustrous he longed to run his hands through it.

She was his wife—he could…

No, he couldn't.

But surely he could greet her with a light touch on her shoulder, a small kiss of greeting on her cheek.

He walked towards her, aware that his legs weren't working properly but reaching her nonetheless.

'You look beautiful, although, in case I didn't tell you, this morning you looked truly magnificent. I am very proud to be your husband.'

That last bit was definitely his head talking, settling his attraction, being firm with it, so the kiss he gave her *was* on her cheek, not those full pink lips that had been tempting him.

'Tonight I have ordered some different delicacies. You ate so little after the ceremony I was sure you would be hungry. These little pastries are lamb with pine nuts and pomegranate syrup, you must try one.'

He passed the plate, and watched her slim fingers lift the pastry and pop it into her mouth. Wanted her to feed him again, so he could take those fingers into *his* mouth, suckle on them—

He offered food, she took it, ate himself, but with tension twisting tighter every moment they spent together.

Surely sharing a meal shouldn't make him want to throw her down on the carpet in the midst of all that food and take her as his wife?

She was talking, but he barely listened, libidinous thoughts blocking out her words.

He wasn't entirely certain his heart was involved but his head surely wasn't!

Had he not listened to his father, not read and

taken in those words around the palace every day of his life?

So where was his head?

Why wasn't it helping?

'I think that is all I can manage,' she said, smiling, he thought shyly, at him. 'Although that yoghurt with the honey and dates and pomegranate seeds was so delicious I could have eaten the whole bowl.'

'Eat it then,' he said, his voice gruff with the mix of emotions within him.

Another smile, more confident now.

'And make a pig of myself? I think not. Pop always told us that the best way to diet was to push yourself away from the table when you've had enough, not stay and finish it because it's there.'

'Then let us take our coffee on the comfortable settee in the loggia. And you can tell me about the man you call Pop.'

She studied him for a moment, as if trying to work out if he was saying something else, but in the end stood, in a smooth, graceful movement that must have been born to her for it was never easily managed by Western women.

So they sat together in the loggia, and talked a little of her upbringing, but she wanted to know more of his.

'It's why I came, after all, to learn about the people and the history of my mother's home.'

Where to start?

He was pondering this, thinking of what he'd already explained about the trade routes through the desert, when she laid a hand on his arms and said, 'Before that, could I ask you something?'

'Anything,' he replied, only just biting back the words 'my love' that had wanted to come out of his mouth.

'Back in my rooms, I rested for a while, half asleep, half dreaming, so I really do not know if it was a dream of a scrap of memory from before the accident… But I thought we were at the beach, my mother, father and myself, and my father was splashing in the shallow water, leaping over the waves as they came in and calling to my mother. Calling her to come in, using her name.'

She paused and looked at his face, as if wondering whether he was following her story.

Then very earnestly she said, 'I know that part is not a dream—I do remember that, and it fits that the beach would have been at Wetherby because we were driving away from the town up winding roads into the hills when the accident occurred.'

Another pause, this one longer, then a smile and a shrug of her slim shoulders, as if deciding she'd go on even if it didn't make much sense.

'Then, in the dream or memory I heard him call, "Come, Nalini, follow your leopard," and it's weird because that made me remember, or think I remembered, that sometimes my mother called my father leopard.'

Lila looked at Tariq, eyes wide, hoping that he might be able to make sense of this confession, and when he didn't speak she added, 'Does it make any sense to you? Could it be possible my mother called my father leopard—I'd felt a tug of memory that night on the path when we nearly encountered one, but couldn't follow the thread—although perhaps it's just nonsense, dreams...'

No response.

Nothing!

And his face had become a graven mask yet again, although earlier it had been warm, and smiling—admiring, even...

Then a long sigh.

Could a sigh sound heartfelt?

Her chest was tight, her breathing erratic, his reaction told her it *had* to mean something to him!

'So it *was* Fahad she went off with,' he said, so quietly he might have been speaking to himself.

Another sigh, and then he added, more strongly now, 'His family, of course, denied it, claiming he had gone to America to study and had met with an accident there, and he did go to America, months before Nalini disappeared. My father's investigators established that much.'

Lila heard the words, so unexpectedly out there she grasped the Ta'wiz, pressing it against her chest.

Had she found her father?

Found a name for him?

Fahad and Nalini—both parents…

Her fingers trembled on her mother's last gift, while her heart beat so rapidly she could barely breathe.

'Are you saying,' she began hesitantly, 'that this Fahad might be my father?'

Had he heard the stress in her voice that he turned and put his hand over hers, easing the pressure of her fingers on the locket, grasping them in a warm engulfing squeeze?

'I'm sorry, this is all too much for you, you've been thrust every which way ever since your arrival. Perhaps you need to rest. The story has waited long enough to be told—it can wait a little longer.'

Lila shook her head.

'No, I need to know. I came to find out. I thought it would take for ever, maybe it might never happen at all, but more than anything I need to know. Who was Fahad?'

'He was the son of a cousin of my father, an

extremely clever boy who grew into a brilliant young man. My father had selected him for great things in government, to be the Minister of Finance, and oversee the setting up of a national banking system. His name, as you may have guessed, means leopard.'

Tariq stopped, wondering just how much more the young woman by his side could take.

Yes, she wanted to know about her family, that was only natural, but details, gossip, hearsay and possibly downright lies—there'd been so many stories told...

'You'll hear the stories, many of them more fairy tales than truth. But one thing is for certain, my father adored him, and had I not been born, he would have been Crown Prince and taken over from my father.'

He paused again. He'd been a child, so what were memories and what were tales, he no longer knew.

'My mother had four daughters before I was born, and then three more. My father refused to believe what he considered was medical mumbo-jumbo, refused to believe that he could possibly be responsible for the sex of his children, so he married Second Mother—your aunt—and continued to produce daughters until Khalil came along. So now he had two sons—an heir and a spare as they say—so Fahad was of less importance to him, but was still adored.'

'Then he disappeared?' Lila asked, her voice husky with emotion.

'Only to America—and by arrangement. Many of our young men go there to study, there or to Europe. We had to catch up on modern ways, learn so much in a short time, it was necessary that the best and brightest went away.'

'And did many disappear?'

Tariq sighed for about the fourth time in what had been a relatively short story, but it was getting late and maybe the rest of the story could wait.

Although maybe not for Lila…

'Did no one keep in touch? Search for them?' she asked.

He turned to see her eyes fixed on his face,

awaiting an answer—an answer as to why no one had ever found her parents.

Found her...

The thought of the orphaned child she'd been, unable to talk, to explain who she was, hurt his chest in a way he'd never felt before, and he wanted to put his arm around her shoulders and draw her close, as much for his comfort as for hers.

But his head stayed headfast!

'I imagine the family provided any number of private investigators with a very good living over many years. And, yes, some of our young men didn't so much disappear as decided to stay where they'd been studying. Some met and married local girls, went into businesses not connected with the family, but they kept in touch, if only sporadically so they hadn't actually disappeared.'

'But Fahad did?'

Tariq nodded.

'Fahad did. As I said, my father sent him to study in America, and from there somehow it was discovered he'd had a holiday in Brazil, then someone had had contact with him in Paris, and his family always swore he'd gone back to the States. But within a year the trail went cold, and the investigators' reports were more padding than information. He had disappeared.'

'But if he left first—left legally with a good excuse for going—then he would have had nothing to do with the theft.'

She sounded despondent, as if she'd have preferred that at the very least her parents had shared the blame.

Or did having two parents who were thieves make her feel worse?

He looked at the woman by his side, and read both excitement and weariness in her face, but the weariness was winning.

'Come,' he said gently, 'I will walk you to your bedroom. There will be time enough tomorrow to talk of these things. We might even find some photos—at least of Fahad—for I'm certain Second Mother would have destroyed all the photos of Nalini.'

He stood up and took Lila's hand, her fingers fitting perfectly into his palm, his hand wanting to hold her for ever.

But now the Fahad business had been raised, he knew she'd want answers.

Could he give them?

He doubted it!

Just because Lila had vague memories of her mother calling her father leopard, did that make the Fahad connection true?

Tariq tried to think, to remember exactly how the events had transpired. First Fared leaving, then, months later he was sure, Nalini.

Lila was silent as they walked back through the apartment to her rooms, but she'd be tired, and on top of that had much to think about.

So he was surprised when she stopped outside her door and turned towards him, rising up on her toes to kiss him lightly on the lips.

'Thank you for all you've done for me today, and thank you, too, for maybe finding my father.'

He put his arms around her, not wanting to let her go.

In fact, what he really wanted to do was throw her over his shoulder and take her into his room next door, there to ravish her until they were both exhausted.

Wouldn't his barbarian ancestors—and hers possibly—have acted that way?

Not if their heads really had always ruled their hearts.

And having grown up believing in his father's dictum, could he change it now?

He returned her kiss, his own a little more insistent, less polite than inviting, caught a sigh from her, faint as a whisper, then she eased away and disappeared through her door.

Into a room that had a connecting door to his!

Did she know that?

CHAPTER TEN

LILA SLIPPED INTO her bedroom, only too aware that the door in the side wall of her bedroom must lead into Tariq's room.

The urge to use that door, to slip through it so she could be held in the safety of his arms, was almost overwhelming.

And, after all, she now knew who she was—or was fairly certain of it.

So why hold back?

You can still leave him if the worst were to happen and Khalil were to die, keep that part of the agreement; she just had to explain that she had not wanted to be with someone until she'd discovered who *she* was.

Surely he would understand that…

But explaining that would be the easy part. Admitting to being a virgin would be totally humiliating. Yes, Karuban men apparently valued virgin brides, but those brides would all be far younger than her, many of them still in their teens.

And what did she know?

What would she do?

Knowledge of physiology and biology was all well and good, but the actual act of sex? And worse still would be how to please him—who told you things like that? Hallie certainly hadn't, although her sex talks had been clear, open and understandable, but as far as Lila could recall, pleasuring your husband hadn't been a topic.

And she'd like to pleasure Tariq...

Feeling saddened and not a little forlorn with her thoughts, she determinedly threw them off. *You're the one who put the embargo on sex in this marriage, so live with it. Head not heart, remember.*

But it had definitely been her head that had added the proviso, mainly because her heart was already lost to the man who was now her husband.

Her head had been very firm about the fact

that it would be so much harder to leave him if they'd been intimate than it would if they remained nothing more than friends.

She peeled off her clothes, wondering as she did so if Tariq was mirroring her movements right next door. She pictured him, broad chested, slabs of muscle beneath pale olive skin, reaching down to peel off his...

She still didn't know what he wore under his gown but he'd been in chinos tonight so he'd be peeling off either jockeys or boxers, revealing—

Knees suddenly weak, she sat down on the bed and held her head in her hands, unable to believe she'd been thinking such carnal thoughts about her husband.

About anyone, for that matter...

But not even the icy blast of water she tortured her body with at the end of the shower could wipe away the images in her mind, and she went to bed, still picturing the man, but now in bed with her, holding her close, whispering things his head probably wouldn't let him.

Sleep came eventually, but she woke unrefreshed, and when Tariq joined her for break-fast in the arbour, he looked little better.

'Why don't you stay at home today?' he said. 'I can send someone over with the injection, and to take the blood for testing to see if the stem cell levels are high enough.'

Lila shook her head.

'No, I'd like to finish the report, and the short clinic trip should be back this afternoon so I'll need to talk to Rani and Sybilla about how it went. I feel I'm letting down the side, lolling around the hospital while the team is out work-ing.'

'You are doing something far more important for my family and the country,' Tariq told her in a no-nonsense voice, his head firmly in con-trol. 'And tomorrow, providing the test results are good, they will take your blood, after which you will have a proper rest, a few days off to recover because for all your casual attitude to what you are doing, it will take a toll on your body.'

Lila was about to ridicule this idea, insisting

it had been nothing, until she remembered the pink sand.

If Khalil died, she would be leaving Karuba and she didn't want to leave without at least seeing the sand her mother had so treasured.

'Could we go to the pink sand?' she asked.

'The pink sand?'

Was Tariq really so surprised?

'You said you'd take me,' she reminded him.

And he smiled.

'Of course we can go to the pink sand. It would be an ideal place for you to rest and relax.'

'You can get away?'

He smiled now.

'I'm the boss, I can get away anytime.'

She returned his smile, although she doubted he took much time off at all—boss or not. She might not have known him long, but knew his dedication was to the hospital and the health and welfare of his people.

A day later, with the blood tests showing her blood was ready to harvest, Lila was taken to a special room, where she had cannulas inserted into each arm, then wrapped in tape and bandages to keep them secure. A line from one led to the machine, which then fed her blood, minus the stem cells, back into her body.

Tariq stalked the passage outside the room, knowing he had no part in this but feeling helpless because of that.

To his surprise, his mother appeared, looking as regal as ever.

'Is Lila all right?' was her first question.

'As far as I know,' he growled in reply.

'Then why do you not sit with her? After all, how boring it must be to sit there for, what—five hours, I believe—with no one to talk to.'

'Maybe she doesn't want to talk to me,' Tariq grumbled, and his mother smiled.

'Then *you* must talk to *her*, and if she is well enough, tell her I would like the pair of you to come to dinner tonight. I know it's not the custom for newlyweds to do much visiting in the first month of their marriage, but I need to talk to you both.'

And on that note, his mother disappeared.

But she'd left him heartened, even emboldened. Lila was his wife, why shouldn't he sit with her?

He entered the room and she smiled as if pleased to see him—or perhaps just pleased to have her boredom relieved...

'I've come to sit with you,' he announced, pulling a chair over so they both had chairs.

He took her hand, what was left of it under the swathed bandages.

'After all, you're doing this for the family, and what's more, I am your husband.'

Lila laughed, a light, amused sound.

'Seems a strange time to be undertaking husbandly duties,' she teased. 'Though I must admit I was bored and it's good to have some company other than a pretty, young male nurse who pops in every now and then to make sure I haven't absconded.'

'Would you like to?' Tariq asked, squeezing her cold fingers in his warm hand.

'Oh, no, I'm happy to be doing this. I know it

may not work, but I'd never have forgiven myself if I hadn't tried.'

'But you barely know us. You don't know Khalil at all,' he protested.

'But he's family,' Lila said simply. 'Not that I wouldn't be happy to give stem cells to a stranger, but when it's family it's special, don't you think?'

'More than special,' Tariq answered, and Lila wondered if they were still talking about the stem cells.

But the conversation soon became general. Lila, with her insatiable need to know everything she could about Karuba, asked questions and Tariq answered, expanding on some things, explaining others.

It made the time pass quickly, so Lila was surprised when Professor Eckert came in to declare himself satisfied with his collection, and to arrange for Lila to be released from the restraints of the cannulas and bandages.

Tariq drove her home, instructing her to rest.

'My mother has invited us for dinner,' he said.

'She wishes to speak to us, but if you feel too tired, I can call it off—make it another day.'

Lila was tempted, but getting to know First Mother better was getting to better understand Karuba, and now she knew who her parents were, she longed to know more about their country.

'I'll be ready,' she told him. 'What time?'

'I'll tap on your door a little before eight,' Tariq replied. 'We'll be dining in the small dining room, but it's a jewel of a room if architecture and antiques interest you.'

She nodded, hoping he'd take the gesture as interest in such things, when all she was really interested in was the man who stood beside her at the door.

Perhaps making love to him would clear the restlessness she now felt constantly when she was in his presence.

Then leaving would be easier, not harder…

But she doubted that was true, so she said goodbye and shut the door, certain she wouldn't sleep. So she was surprised when Sousa woke her a little after seven.

'Come,' her friend said, 'You will be late and First Mother hates lateness. You should wear that emerald tunic we bought in the shops at the hotel. The trousers were too long for you, but I have taken up the waist so none of the pattern was lost. The colour is ravishing against your skin, perhaps the best colour of all.'

Was Sousa saying this to make her feel better?

The sleep had left her mind fogged and muzzy, but the shower should clear it. In the end she stood under the hot spray for so long she had to hurry to be ready for Tariq's knock.

Which came, as she'd expected it to, at exactly one minute to eight.

'Very glamorous!' he said, as he took in her appearance.

Lila waved away the compliment, although inwardly it pleased her.

'It's all Sousa's doing. She tells me what to wear and when to wear it and I just go along with it.'

'No, it is the beauty of the person within the clothes that makes them special.'

Startled by the compliment, Lila looked up into his eyes, seeking something—truth?

'I mean it,' he said quietly. 'I may not have known you long, but I do know you are beautiful, inside and out. As your mother was...'

She wanted to protest, But my mother was a thief who risked another man's life to get what she wanted, but deep within she knew his words were true, that her mother had been a beautiful person, inside and out.

'So why? How?' she said instead, the pleasure of his compliment now dimmed by the past.

He clasped his arms loosely around her and drew her towards him—close but not touching.

'We do not know, and may never know—can you live with that?'

Lila thought about it for a moment, then nodded slowly.

'Yes, I believe I can, for my memories of her are of a warm, loving, vibrant, laughing being. I will never let the stories taint that.'

'Because you won't be here to hear them?'

His voice was very serious, dark somehow?

'Not if Khalil dies,' she said softly. 'You know as well as I do—better even—that the stories would undermine anything good you wished to do, and diminish your achievements.'

The words were a little shaky, for standing like this, so close to the man she loved, the surge of desire, to have him in her arms, to have him take her as his own, was almost overwhelming.

'We will be late,' she whispered, and wondered if he felt it too, for his hold on her tightened before he sighed and she was able to move away.

Tariq watched as Lila gazed around the room his mother called the small dining room. True, the table would seat only twelve but it was a French antique and shone with years of polish. A large chandelier, another of his mother's purchases from France, hung above it, while the walls were draped with tapestries, the floor covered with rich Persian carpets.

His mother welcomed them and drew them to the small area at one end of the room where guests could mingle or sit quietly and have a drink before dinner.

'You will have juice,' First Mother said to Lila as she led her forward, and Tariq, seeing his mother in full regal mode, knew something was afoot.

Poor Lila must be wondering what had happened, for his mother had been pleasant, and quite human, at their other brief meetings.

The initial chat was general, and, although he could see Lila's fingers trembling on the delicate crystal glass, she held her own, answering politely when questioned, listening politely when being...instructed...

Then First Mother rose.

'We will talk as we eat,' she declared, and as if by magic servants appeared with food, spreading it out at one end of the table then slipping away on silent feet.

'You, Lila, will sit here beside me,' their hostess said, 'and, Tariq, you will take the other side. I wish to speak with you both, but do not want staff present. Please help yourselves to what you want and enjoy the meal.'

It was an unmistakeable order, however quietly spoken, and they both obeyed, Tariq offering dishes first to his mother and then to Lila.

But although the food was delicious, the main dish tender chicken in a honey and raisin sauce, with couscous to absorb the gravy, and tiny vegetables—eggplant, tomatoes and peppers—to complement the dish, he ate little.

Lila was more valiant, tasting everything, complimenting his mother on how delicious it was, stopping only when his mother put down her fork.

'I wish to talk to you of love,' she announced, startling Tariq, and Lila too, from the look of bemusement on her face. 'When two hearts love it is a truly wonderful thing, and I have lived long enough to believe that it is also very rare.'

They both stared at her in silence, until Lila found her voice.

'You are talking about two particular hearts?' she asked, and First Mother nodded.

'I am, child. I am talking about two young people who fell in love many years ago. I was sad at the time, for I had realised the love I felt for my husband wasn't returned, but seeing the young couple, seeing the light in their eyes, the joy of their smiles, the careful attempts to not show how they felt about each other, that brought me a little happiness, because it confirmed for me that the heart *could* rule the head in terms of love.'

It dawned slowly on Lila, and even then she wondered if she should ask the question.

But this was why she'd come to Karuba. She had to set aside the pain in her own heart that knew its love was not returned.

'Was it my parents? Was it their love you saw?'

The regal head nodded.

'But it was impossible, you see. Fahad was to be married to someone else, and my husband was already looking for a bridegroom for your mother. He was also writing "The Head Must Rule the Heart" all over the palace walls to punish me for wanting love from him, heart love, so I knew how dangerous their love was.'

Lila was wondering just how hard this must

have been for her parents when Tariq asked his mother, 'But if it was obvious to you, how did no one else see it?'

First Mother smiled sadly.

'No one else was hurting the way I was. You must realise I was hurting for love at that time, so I was attuned to it.'

She paused, then added very quietly, 'As I still am, for still I love my husband and long for his heart to be mine.'

They sat in silence for a while, Lila wanting reach out to the older woman, to show her sympathy, which she was pretty sure would be rejected. First Mother was nothing if not strong.

'So I helped them,' she said at last.

Lost in other dreams of love—*her* heart's love—it took Lila a moment to realise First Mother had spoken again.

'You helped them?' Tariq echoed.

First Mother reached out and touched the Ta'wiz that hung around Lila's neck.

'That was mine, you see, but while it would always remind them of home it wasn't enough. I knew my husband would hire people to find them so they would need money to disappear successfully, to get false documentation, to travel to different places to cover their tracks. My husband made it easy by sending Fahad to America to study, then Nalini only had to wait until enough time had passed that her disappearance wouldn't be connected to him. He wrote to her every day, in letters addressed to me, and I think she wrote back just as often.'

'But the jewellery?' Lila asked, hoping at last to find out exactly what had happened. 'How did she get that?'

For a long moment she thought First Mother wasn't going to answer, but when she did, it was to surprise them both.

'I got it for her,' she said. 'As you now know, I was suffering one-sided love, but there was someone else who also suffered. The Keeper of the Treasury was my husband's youngest brother, and he had loved me for a long time. He knew I was unhappy, so when I asked him for a favour, for him to bring some jewels to me, he thought I was escaping myself and did it, although he knew he would be punished.'

'Didn't that bother you, him being punished? Lila asked, while her heart gave a little skip of joy that her mother had been exonerated.

'I knew he'd be banished, and in truth I thought that would be good for him. To get away from me, you see, because one-sided love, as I'd found out, is not only painful but it is dangerous. He has done well and I think found happiness. At least he married and had children and now grand-children.'

'But this is a secret you've kept for so long, why reveal it now?' Tariq asked, and his mother smiled at him.

'Because your wife, Nalini's daughter, shouldn't be tainted by something in the past, something for which Nalini was completely blameless.'

'So you will tell my father?' Tariq asked, and the regal head nodded once again.

'*And* his other wife, who must be stopped from telling stories and spreading gossip about a woman who did no wrong.'

Her mother, and she would be exonerated! Lila could only shake her head, excitement stirring in the pit of her stomach at the thought that she no longer needed the proviso of leaving him should Khalil die.

She could be his wife in every way.

If he wanted her…

But that thought failed to dampen her imagination as she pictured what might lie ahead.

Tariq's kisses, Tariq's hands on her body, Tariq—

Oh!

How embarrassing, but she'd have to…

She'd have to tell him!

CHAPTER ELEVEN

THEY WALKED OUT through the rose arbour, side by side, close but not touching. Tariq looked at the words written on the walls, and forced his head to rule his heart, although it caused him physical pain.

'So now you know both parents, your mother's been exonerated, and you have given Khalil your stem cells, I would not keep you here if you wished to go.'

'Go?' It was little more than a sigh in the night air, but the next words were stronger, even incredulous. 'You want me to go?'

He took her hand.

'There is nothing I want less,' he whispered, and realised his heart had won the battle.

Now he led her to the labyrinth, something he'd always thought of as a fancy hedge of no particular meaning, walking with her down the winding paths until they reached the middle.

There he turned to her, and saw her face, gilded by the moonlight, a slightly puzzled frown marring the smoothness of her forehead.

'This is the centre of the labyrinth so I can make a wish?' he asked, resting his hand against her cheek, unable to not touch her but fearing where anything more intimate could lead.

'Yes, but you don't tell wishes,' she said, looking steadily into his eyes.

Trying to tell him something?

'I'm sure you can when they've been granted,' he said, and she smiled.

'Okay,' she admitted, 'I wished with all my heart that I'd find out who my parents were.'

'And that's come true, which proves to me that what I wish for now might also come true.'

Her frown deepened.

'What do you have to wish for?' she said. 'You know your family, you have all this...' She waved her hand around. 'What more could you possibly want?'

'Love?' he said, as his head gave in completely. 'The kind of love your parents knew—the love of two hearts.'

He paused, wondering if he'd gone too far, for she was trembling now.

He drew her close and kissed her hair, whispering from his heart, 'I love you more than I ever thought to love anyone. You have brought me joy. You fill me with admiration for your caring nature, your kindness to all you meet, and the strength that brought you here in search of your parents. They all add up to an inner beauty that almost, but not quite, outshines your outward beauty, your laughing eyes, your soft rose lips, the feel of you against my body. I have disobeyed my father's dictum and I am sorry, but I do love you with my heart as well as with my head.'

She raised her face to his, wonderment and something else shining in her eyes.

'You love me?' she whispered, as though the idea was too much for her to handle.

'More than life itself! You have stolen into my heart, and you will always be there.'

He tightened his arms around her, drawing her closer, his heart racing as he waited, hoping to hear she loved him, fearful she might not...

'As you will be in mine,' she finally said, and he could breathe again. 'I may not have known you long but I love you for the kind, generous, caring, unselfish man you are, and for your gentleness and tenderness, your understanding.'

'And my body?' he teased as his blood fizzed with joy, and he drew her even closer to seal their love with a kiss.

'So, what's left to wish for?' she teased, when they finally drew apart to take a breath.

'I think we both know that,' he said.

'Do your labyrinth rules allow a joint wish?'

'I'm sure they could,' she said.

'Then we wish for a long life together, with the love that binds us bringing joy and light and laughter every day.'

They walked back through the gardens to Tariq's apartments, hand in hand, but wordless, as if the words spoken already had been of such magnitude there were none left to say.

Tariq felt the warmth of the woman by his side, picked up a faint scent from her shining hair, wanted desperately to hold her, kiss her, learn her body through all his senses, yet something held him back.

She'd had a big day, and could well be exhausted, yet he doubted she'd object if he kissed her, tempted her with teasing touches, and eventually led—or maybe carried—her into his bedroom.

But was that fair?

Eckert, damn his soul, had said she should rest, but tomorrow?

And it occurred to him exactly what to do tomorrow. Tomorrow he would give her a very special gift—a visit to the pink sands—and there he'd make her his.

Excited now, he walked more swiftly for there were plans to be made, orders to be given, things to be put in place.

'Are you hurrying to get away from me?' she asked, and he realised she was having trouble keeping up.

He stopped and turned towards her, taking her face in his hands, kissing her soft lips.

'Never!' he said, 'Never.'

And found he truly meant it.

She met his kiss with one of her own, her tongue teasing at his lips, tangling with his, her body pressed so close they could already be one.

He ran his fingers through her hair, kissed her eyelids, temple, chin, covered her face with kisses while her hands roved his head, his neck, his back, learning the contours of him through her fingertips.

She was trembling now, his own body hard, both wanting yet restrained by their presence in the garden where their every move could be being watched.

And he thought again of his idea and knew it was right.

'Not tonight, my love,' he said, easing her away from his body. 'But tomorrow. Tell Sousa we will leaved at nine, and that we're going to the desert.'

A tiny furrow appeared between her eyebrows

as if his words had disappointed her, so he drew her close again.

'You must rest tonight,' he said, 'and if you were in my bed, there'd be no chance of that. So I shall escort you to your room like a proper gentleman, kiss you goodnight, and see you in the morning.'

Except he did more than kiss her goodnight, he told her of his love, and heard with a fast-beating heart her own confession of the love she felt for him.

Lila lay in bed, exhausted but finding sleep elusive. In her mind she replayed the conversation over dinner, and hugged Tariq's parting words to herself, but niggling away inside her was the silly virginity thing, and the question of how and when to bring it up—if at all—kept her awake long into the night.

In the end, it was easy, because Tariq's gift the next day was so extraordinary, so special, so much an avowal of his love that other matters faded into insignificance.

Or almost.

They flew in his small helicopter, out across the sand, along the shoreline until ahead she could see a vision of pink.

'Pink sand?' she asked, and Tariq smiled at her.

'Pink flamingos—the flamingo lake.'

'The sand is near it? Is the sand pink because it reflects the flamingos?'

'Wait and see,' he teased, settling the little helicopter down a small distance from yet another low-slung tent, carpets spread in front of it, fat cushions heaped on them, and a small fire burning at the edge.

They walked, hand in hand again, towards the tent, and looking down Lila realised the sand *was* pink. She knelt and scooped up a handful then turned her back on the lake and the graceful birds, and held the sand in shadow.

Still pink, the sand, so not a reflection at all.

'Disbeliever!' Tariq teased, and she smiled at him.

'Thank you,' she said, letting the sand run through her fingers. 'Thank you from the bottom of my heart, because now I feel my journey is complete.'

'Not quite complete,' he said, his voice husky with desire.

She knew she was blushing, heat reddening her cheeks, but as he led her to the cushions on the carpet, she knew the time had come.

'I need to talk to you,' she said, and saw surprise shadow the desire in his eyes.

'It's a little embarrassing but best got out of the way and if you could understand that I had to study hard at school to get into medicine, then study hard there, and at the same time look for my parents, and while I had boyfriends, they didn't ever last because I was too intense, too serious, or too intent maybe on finding out my story, so although I know all the theory, I—'

The words had come out in a rush, and suddenly dried up.

Tariq was now obviously perplexed, as if trying to replay all she'd said in his head. He was frowning now, so she plunged into speech once more.

'And it was more than that,' she said. 'It was

to do with who I was, and a feeling I had that I couldn't really give myself to anyone until I knew who I was.'

There, that should make it plain, but looking into Tariq's face she wondered if it had.

Then suddenly he smiled, and drew her into his arms, lifting her off the ground and swinging her around.

'Are you telling me, my wife, that you're a virgin?'

Blushing rosily again, she nodded, and began to apologise, but he kissed the words away.

'My precious woman, my flower, my bride, and soon my wife, do you not realise how rare a gift you bring me? To know that you are mine and only mine is very, very special. And now our union must be gentle, and you must guide me if I'm rushing you, for I want it to be as great an experience for you as it will be for me.'

He carried her into the tent, where more soft cushions were piled on carpets, and stood with her in front of him, first kissing her, then touching her, her arms, her waist, hands sliding down her legs, then up, brushing lightly against her womanhood, and pausing briefly on her breasts.

Then slowly he removed her tunic, lifting it over her head, so she stood naked but for a bra from the waist up.

'You're allowed to undress me as well,' he teased, holding out his arms so she could lift his robe from his body, but his height and her nerves made that impossible so he stripped it off and stood before her in a snowy white sarong tied around his waist.

Not boxer shorts then, Lila realised, and knew the thought was more hysteria than anything else, for this slow undressing, their closeness and light touches already had flames burning inside her.

So aware of moving slowly, Tariq curbed the heat within him, and lifted this very special woman, to set her down in the soft cushions, there to fondle her, excite her, remove the rest of her clothes and his, so skin to skin they could communicate without words.

But touches said enough, hers shy at first, then growing bolder, and while he traced his fingers up her inner leg and moved them between her thighs, he heard her whimper with need, and felt her hands tighten about him.

He nipped at one rosy breast and heard her gasp, then felt her body move as the sensations he was creating in her told her that there was more—that she *needed* more.

She was moist and ready, but still he moved slowly, although her hand had found his hardness and was teasing it, feeling the skin, the length, the tip where moisture beaded.

'There'll be a little pain—and if I'm going too fast, tell me to stop.'

He whispered the words in her ear as her hands guided him towards her moistness, then suddenly they were joined, and, yes, a wince of pain, but he moved slowly, letting her catch the rhythm that was as old as the sands on which they lay, as old as time itself.

He felt her shudder as she reached her peak, and finished with her, holding her tightly, staying joined as he rolled onto his side, taking her with him so he could look into her eyes.

'It will get better,' he said gently, but she smiled and pressed her finger to his lips.

'I know it will, but that was special and I thank you.'

He held her tight, this woman who had swept into his life, wearing the ancient Ta'-wiz, returning it and good fortune to his country.

And now she was truly his.

Later, they walked on the sand, nibbled on delicacies packed in hampers inside the tent, and that night made love beneath the light of a billion bright stars.

'But none as bright as my star,' Tariq murmured, tucking Lila close to his body and drawing a quilt over them as the night air grew cold.

At dawn the flamingos took off in a vast flying carpet of pink, circled above the lake, then settled back down, to prod and poke among the weeds.

Tariq made coffee in a silver pot, setting it above the fire that had burned steadily through the night.

He found pastries and other delicacies in the hampers and fed his wife, his woman, who, in turn, held her coffee cup to his lips so they could drink together.

But as they prepared to leave—they both needed to return to work—Tariq produced a small parcel, and handed it to Lila.

'A wedding gift,' he said, quietly and very seriously, so her fingers shook as she undid the wrappings, and tears rolled down her cheeks when she saw the box.

It was as like her mother's as she could remember, burnished wood with silver-and-gold filigree work all around it. She opened it and he knelt at her feet and passed the pink sand up to her, then she, too knelt, to kiss him as her throat was too tight for words.

Later, with the box full of sand and clutched firmly in one hand, she recovered enough to say, 'But I have no gift for you.'

And he smiled, and held her close, and said, 'You gave me your gift last night, my love. I could have thought of no greater one.'

And standing on the pink sand by the flamingo lake, they held each other, and kissed, not passionately this time, although passion wasn't ever far away, but with a quiet promise to each other, that this was how it would always be...

EPILOGUE

It was a day of celebration. Flags and bunting festooned the city while in the palace Lila tried desperately to control the excitement of her children. Fahad, now twelve, would be going with his father to the men's side of the wedding, while the twins, Nalini and Barirah, at ten, would be allowed to attend with the women.

Now dressed and ready to be gone, they were chasing each other through the corridors of the apartment, or were, until Hallie appeared from a doorway and called them to order, suggesting they wait outside until their parents were ready to depart.

Lila had to smile. Hallie and Pop, both still vibrant with life in spite of their age, had flown over for the wedding, insisting, when Lila had invited them, that they'd missed one wedding in Karuba and had no intention of missing another.

And although they had only been here a few days, the children were already taking far more notice of Hallie when she spoke than they did of their mother. As for Pop, they followed him around the gardens, asking questions about Australia, a country they'd all visited many times but were still fascinated by.

At times Lila wondered where all the time had gone, yet marvelled that her love and Tariq's had never weakened, if anything growing stronger as they raised their family, and worked together at the hospital, Lila still doing the clinic runs, often taking the children with her so they got to know the tribal people and better understood their heritage.

But today was Khalil's day!

He'd not only recovered but become a strong and handsome man, taking over as Sheikh when his father had died five years ago, and already reaping high praise for his leadership and wisdom.

'Because of your stem cells,' Tariq would tease her, but Lila believed it had been his own inner strength and courage that had pulled him through his illness, and those same qualities made him the great man he'd become.

'What are you thinking?'

Tariq's voice still sent a shiver down her spine, and his touch, as he came up to stand beside her, sent a thrill through her blood.

'Not regretting we didn't have a grand wedding like this one?'

She turned to him, kissing him lightly on the lips.

'Not for one second,' she assured him. 'Our wedding was perfect, just like our life and our love.'

'Perfect!' Tariq echoed, putting his arms around her and holding her lightly in his arms. 'As are you, my love.'

'And you,' she echoed, for just as they'd wished in the labyrinth all those years ago, their lives had been filled with happiness, their love growing deeper every year.

* * * * *

If you enjoyed this story, check out these other great reads from Meredith Webber

A FOREVER FAMILY FOR THE ARMY DOC
A SHEIKH TO CAPTURE HER HEART
THE MAN SHE COULD NEVER FORGET
THE ONE MAN TO HEAL HER

All available now!

MILLS & BOON®
Large Print Medical

December

January

February